EASTERN MOUNTAINS
RAT CREATURE TEMPLE
CONKLE'S HOLLOW
UPPER PAWA
PAWA
PRAYER STONE HILL
TANEN GARD
FLINT RIDGE
THE GREAT BASIN
PAWA ROAD
ATHEIA
GULCH
SINNER'S ROCK
MC

Dreaming of Harvestar

ACCLAIM FOR JEFF SMITH'S

Named an all-time top ten graphic novel by **Time** *magazine.*

"As sweeping as the 'Lord of the Rings' cycle, but much funnier." —*Andrew Arnold,* **Time.com**

★*"This is first-class kid lit: exciting, funny, scary, and resonant enough that it will stick with readers for a long time."* —**Publishers Weekly**, *starred review*

"One of the best kids' comics ever." —**Vibe** *magazine*

"**BONE** *is storytelling at its best, full of endearing, flawed characters whose adventures run the gamut from hilarious whimsy . . . to thrilling drama."*
—**Entertainment Weekly**

"[This] sprawling, mythic comic is spectacular."
—**SPIN** *magazine*

"Jeff Smith's cartoons are irresistible. Every gorgeous sweep of his brush speaks volumes."
—*Frank Miller, creator of* **Sin City**

"Jeff Smith can pace a joke better than almost anyone in comics." —*Neil Gaiman, author of* Coraline

"I love BONE! BONE *is great!"*
—*Matt Groening, creator of* The Simpsons

"Every one of the zillion characters has a unique set of personality traits and flaws and dreams that are developed amid the pandemonium."
—*Kyle Baker,* Plastic Man *cartoonist*

"BONE *moves from brash humor to gripping adventure in a single panel."* —*ALA* Booklist

"BONE *is a comic-book sensation. . . . [It] is a classic of writer-artist craftsmanship not to be missed."*
—Comics Buyer's Guide

OTHER ***BONE*** BOOKS

Out from Boneville

The Great Cow Race

Eyes of the Storm

The Dragonslayer

Rock Jaw: Master of the Eastern Border

Old Man's Cave

Ghost Circles

Treasure Hunters

BONE

Crown of Horns

By Jeff Smith

with color by Steve Hamaker

graphix

An Imprint of

SCHOLASTIC

This book is for Paul Pope and Terry Moore

Library of Congress Catalog Card Number 9568403.

ISBN-13 978-0-439-70631-5 — ISBN-10 0-439-70631-9

ISBN 0-439-70632-7 (paperback)

ACKNOWLEDGMENTS

Harvestar Family Crest designed by Charles Vess

Map of *The Valley* by Mark Crilley

Color by Steve Hamaker

20 19 18 17 16 15 14 13 12 11 16 17 18 19

First Scholastic edition, February 2009

Book design by David Saylor

Printed in Malaysia 108

CONTENTS

CHAPTER ONE THE DUNGEON & THE PARAPET

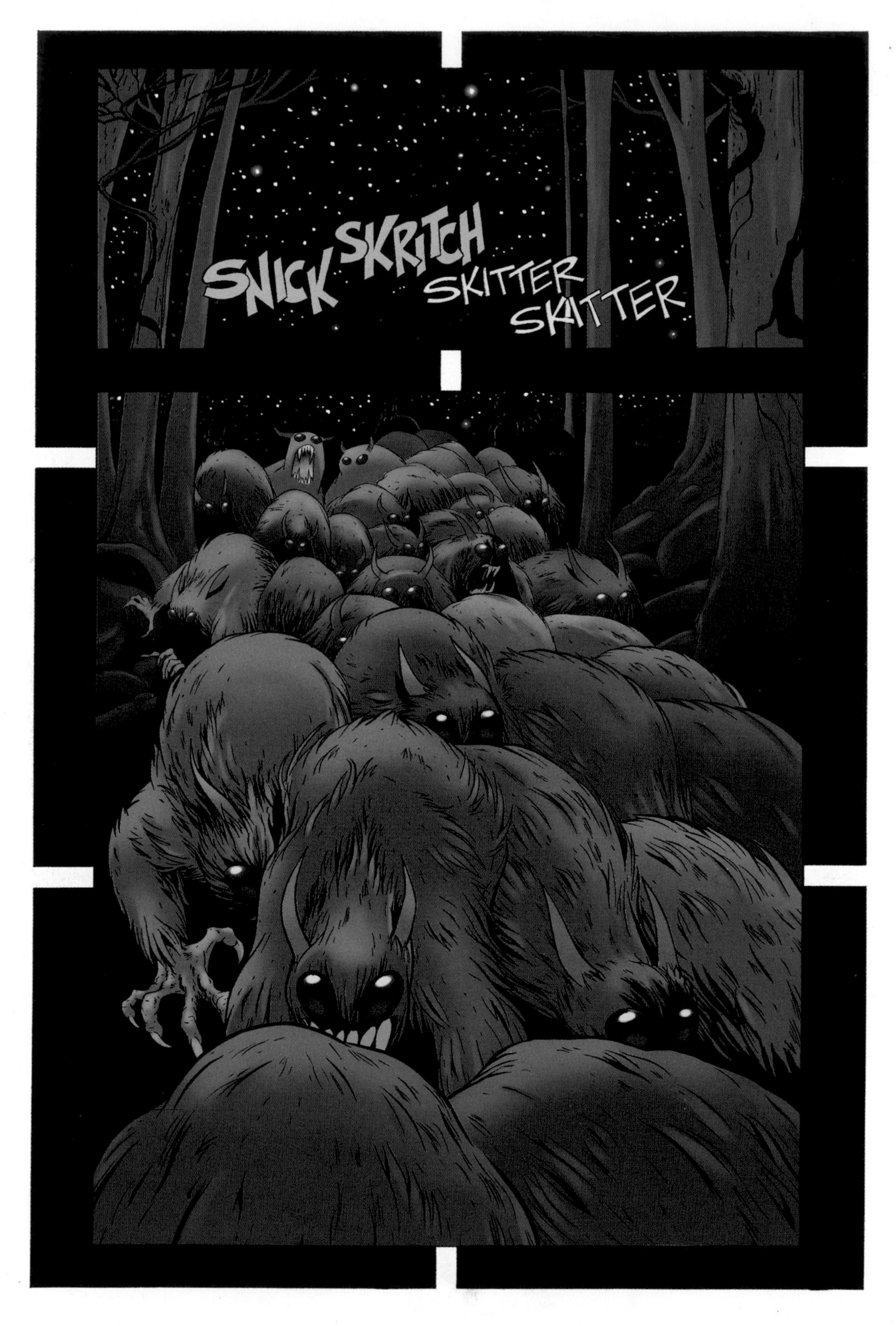
SNICK SKRITCH
SKITTER
SKITTER

THEY'RE COMING - -
RUN - -
WHAT ABOUT THE COURTYARD?
THEY'VE GONE TO JOIN THEM ON THE WALLS!
FILL EVERY VESSEL WITH WATER!
THE VILLAGE IS LOST.
THE GATE CANNOT HOLD MUCH LONGER.
ONLY WHAT YOU CAN CARRY . . . .
THEY'VE ENTERED THE COURTYARD.
HURRY! TAKE THE CHILD!

THORN, WAKE UP!
YOU'RE DREAMING!
..MOTHER.....
..WHERE ARE WE GOING?

THERE IS FIGHTING IN THE STREETS - -
YOUR MAJESTY, YOU MUST LEAVE THE CITY.
WE WON'T MAKE IT. THE RAT CREATURES ARE CLOSING IN!
I CAN TAKE THEM TO MY SISTER.
THAT WON'T BE EASY- - BUT WE HAVE NO OTHER CHOICE. I WILL LEAD THE MONSTERS AWAY, WHILE YOU MAKE FOR THE SECRET PATH.
FOLLOW BRIAR! SHE WILL DELIVER YOU TO ROSE AND THE RED DRAGON!
MOTHER!
YOU ARE SAFE! WHERE IS MY GRANDDAUGHTER?
SHE IS HERE. LET US HURRY TO DEREN GARD.

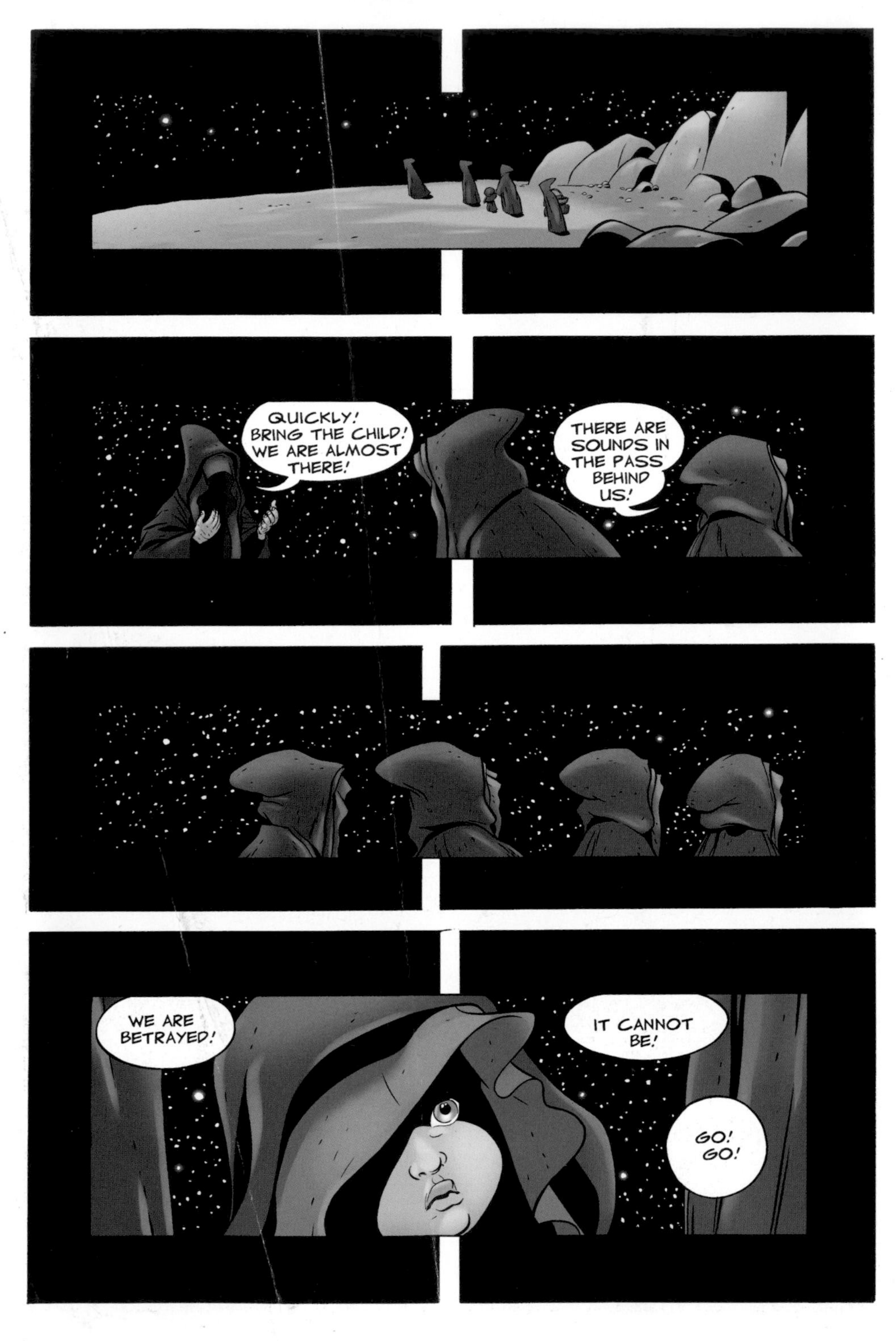
QUICKLY! BRING THE CHILD! WE ARE ALMOST THERE!
THERE ARE SOUNDS IN THE PASS BEHIND US!
WE ARE BETRAYED!
IT CANNOT BE!
GO! GO!

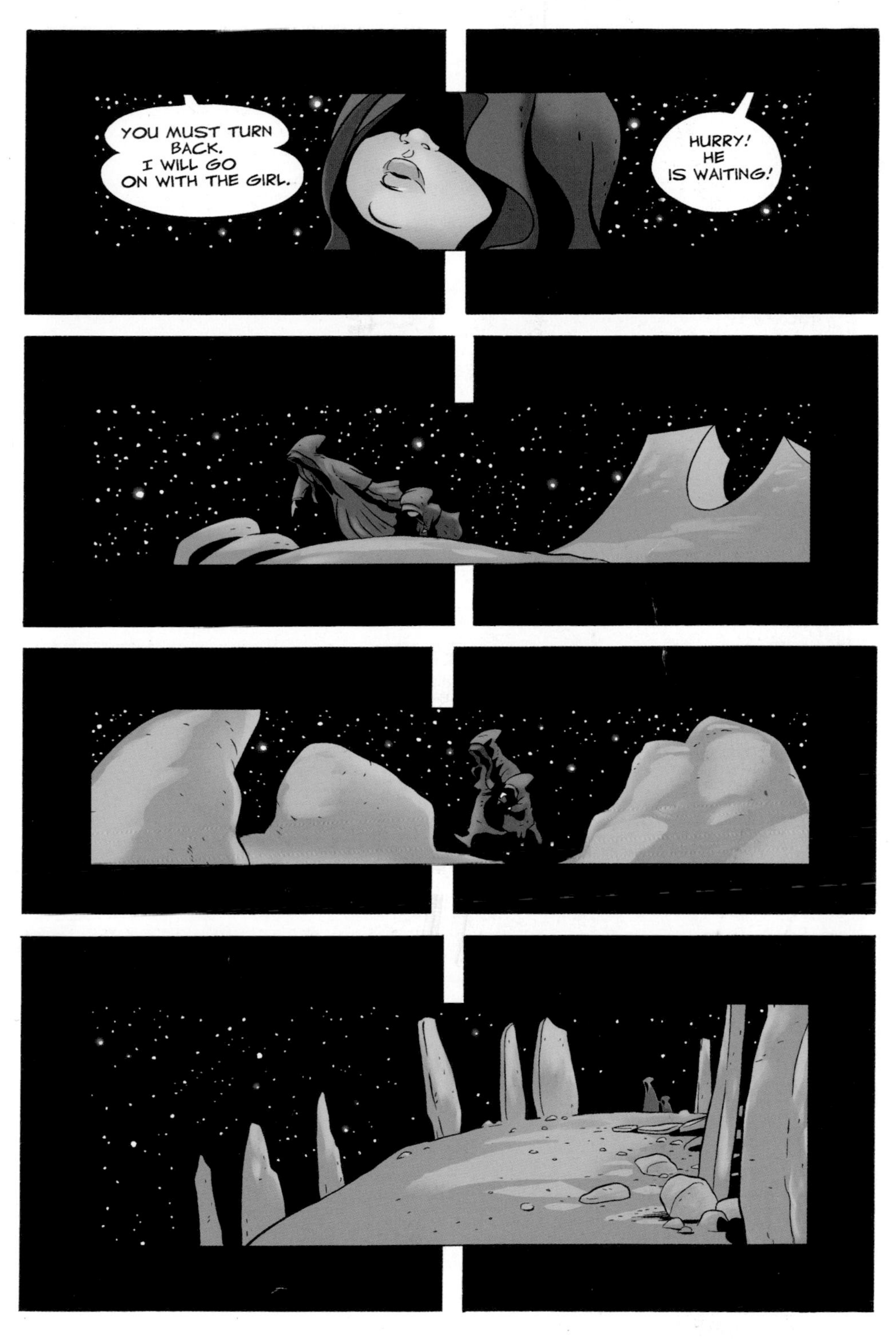
YOU MUST TURN BACK. I WILL GO ON WITH THE GIRL.
HURRY! HE IS WAITING!

BE STILL, LITTLE ONE.

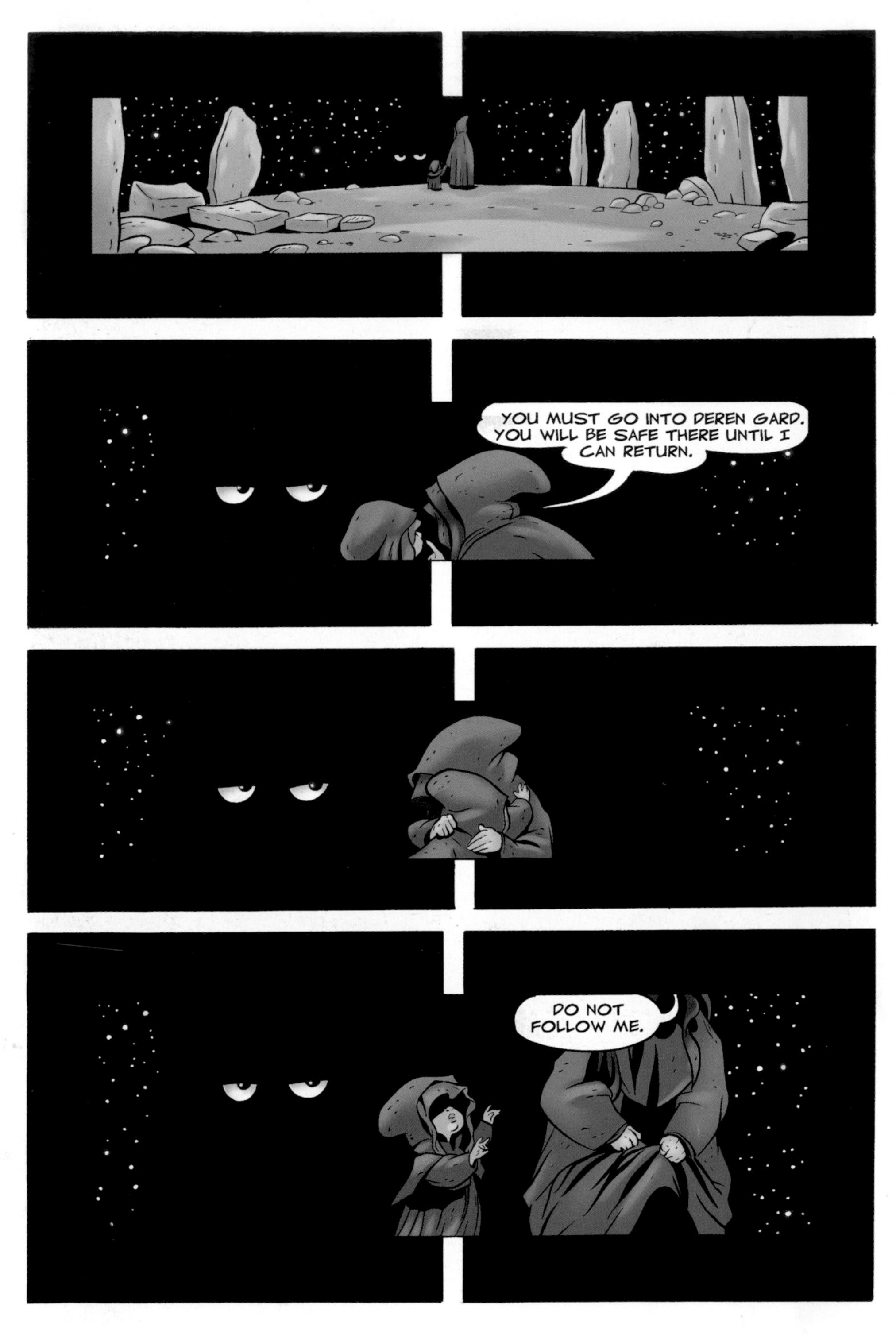
YOU MUST GO INTO DEREN GARD. YOU WILL BE SAFE THERE UNTIL I CAN RETURN.
DO NOT FOLLOW ME.

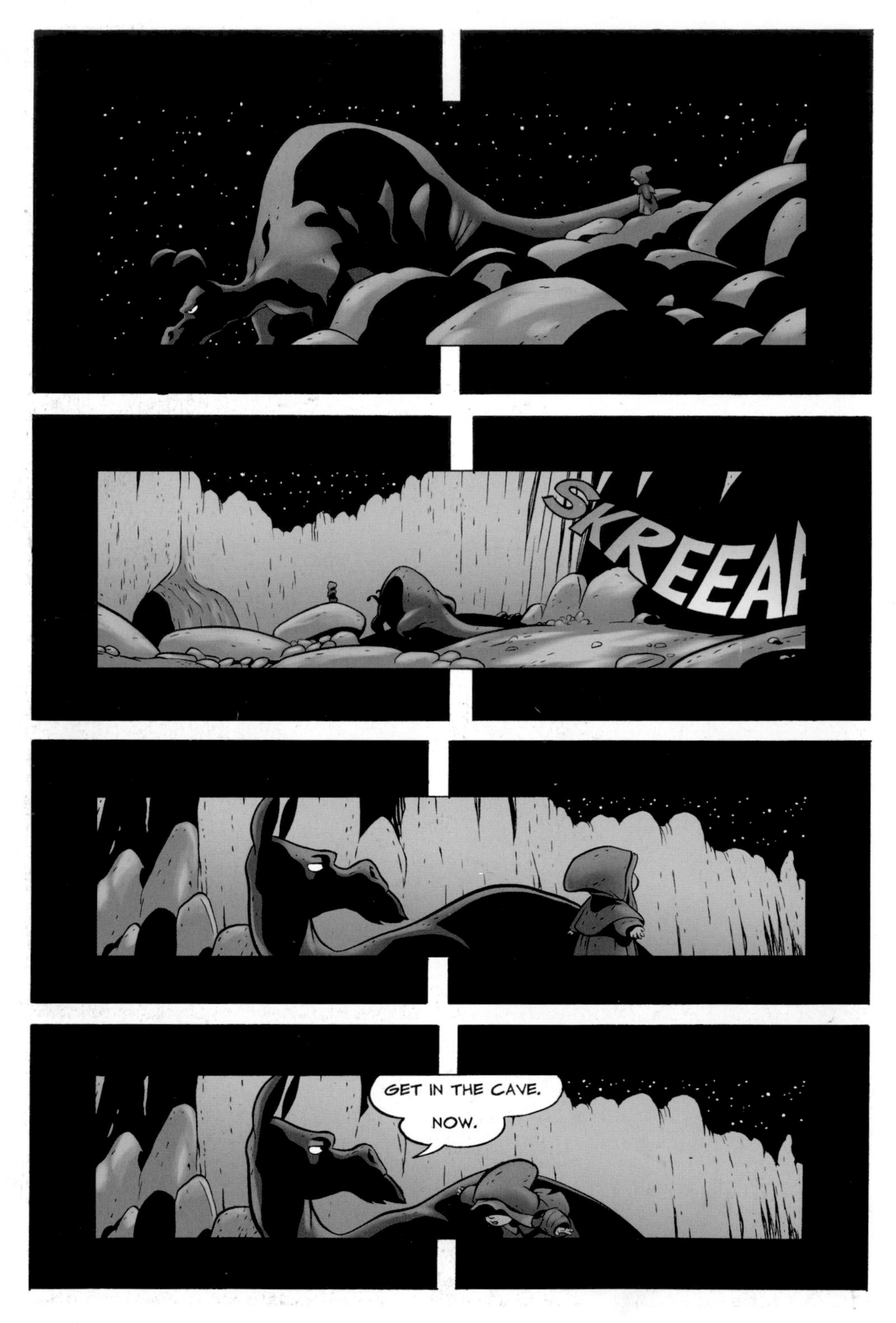
SKREEAH
GET IN THE CAVE.
NOW.

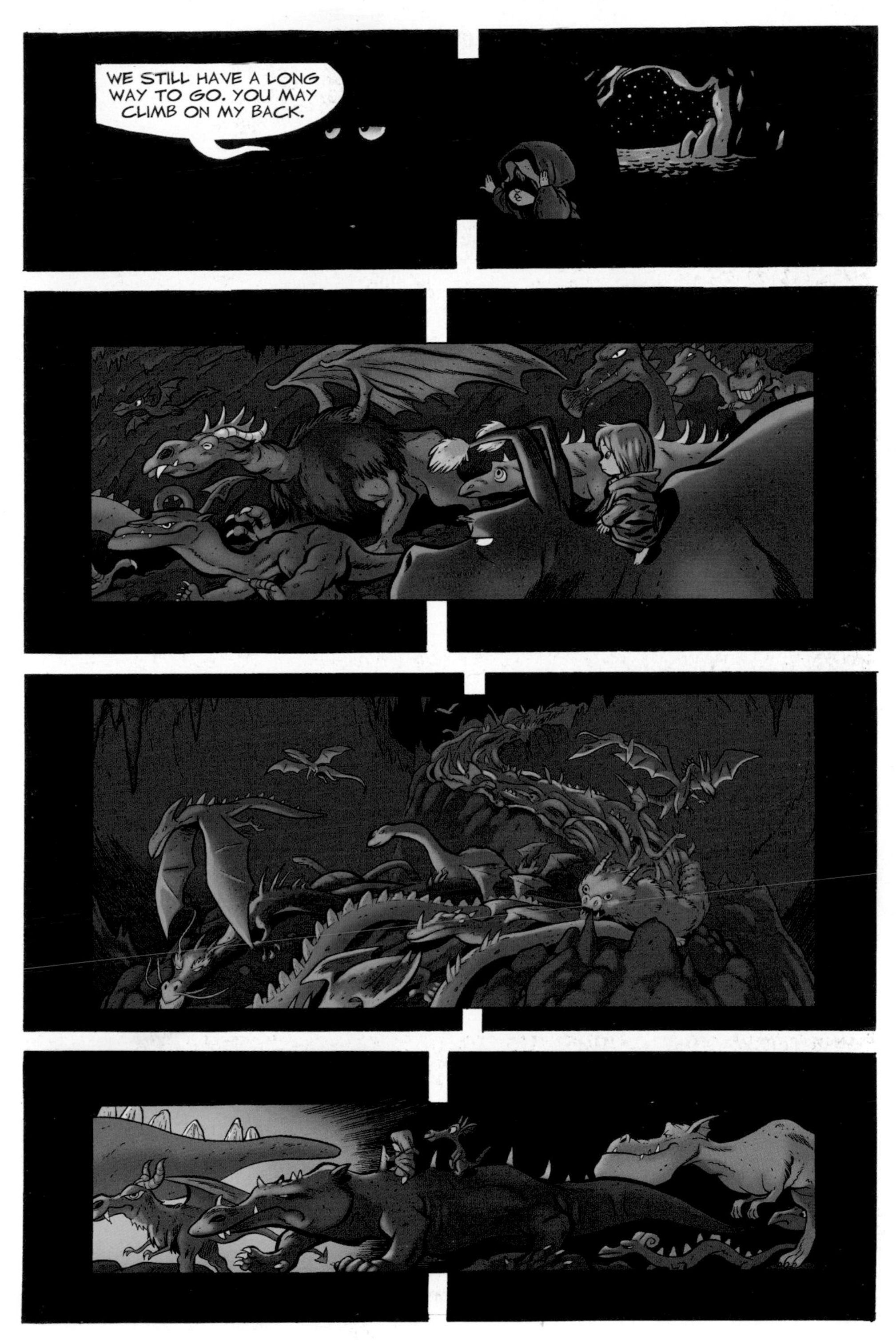
WE STILL HAVE A LONG WAY TO GO. YOU MAY CLIMB ON MY BACK.

COME HERE, THORN.

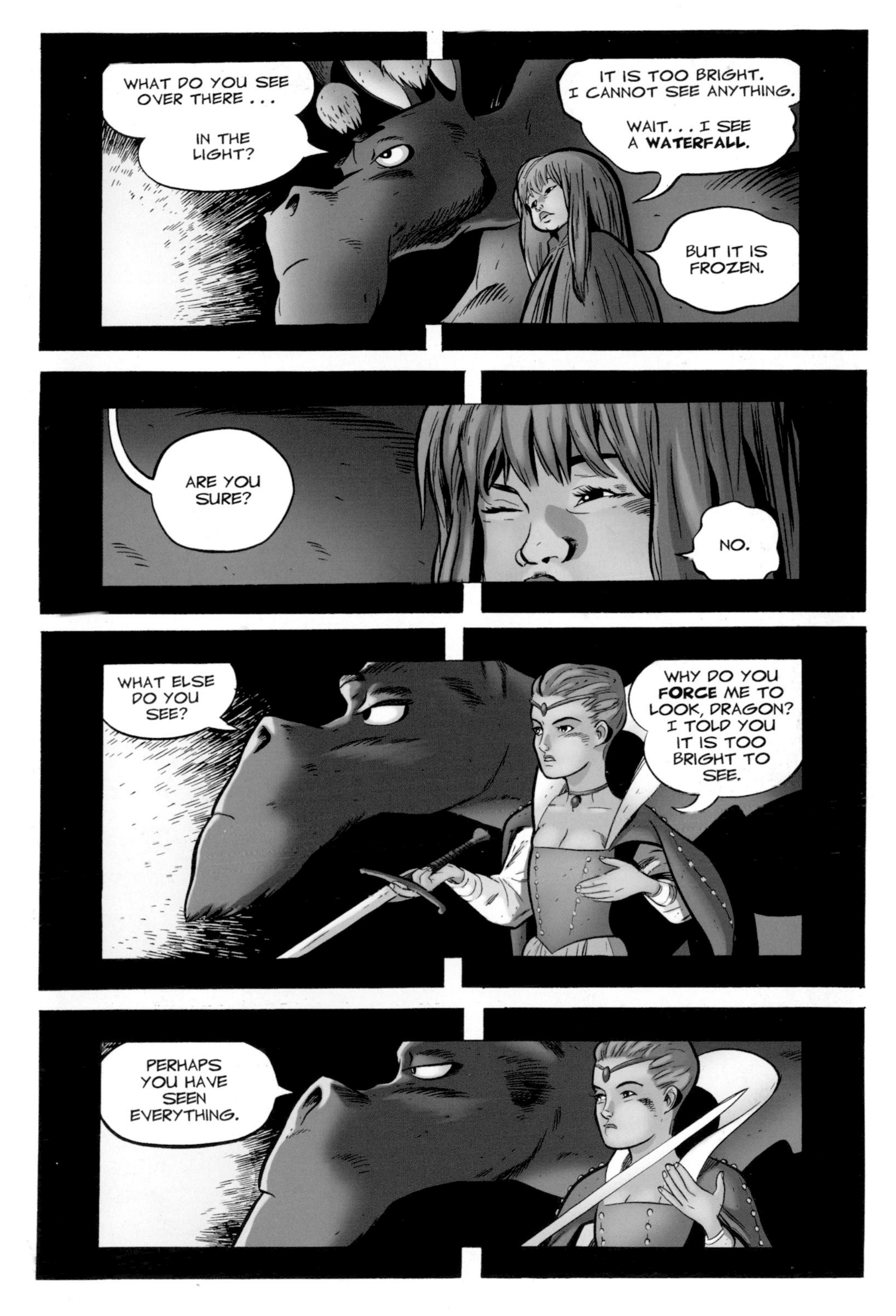
WHAT DO YOU SEE OVER THERE . . .
IN THE LIGHT?
IT IS TOO BRIGHT. I CANNOT SEE ANYTHING.
WAIT. . . I SEE A **WATERFALL.**
BUT IT IS FROZEN.
ARE YOU SURE?
NO.
WHAT ELSE DO YOU SEE?
WHY DO YOU **FORCE** ME TO LOOK, DRAGON? I TOLD YOU IT IS TOO BRIGHT TO SEE.
PERHAPS YOU HAVE SEEN EVERYTHING.

THORN.
WAKE UP, PLEASE.
MOTHER?
YOU MUST HURRY.
SEEK THE CROWN of HORNS.

THORN, ARE YOU AWAKE?
WHA - - ?
WHAT HAPPENED?
TARSIL'S SOLDIERS BEAT THE TAR OUT OF US AND LOCKED US IN THE DUNGEON. YOU MUST'VE BLACKED OUT OR SOMETHING.
I HAD THE DREAM AGAIN.
SAME ONE YOU'VE HAD SINCE YOU WERE A KID?
YEAH. THE ONE WHERE MY PARENTS GIVE ME TO THE DRAGONS.
IT WAS WEIRD . . . FOR THE FIRST TIME EVER, I SAW MY MOTHER'S FACE . . .

BUT WHEN THE DRAGONS TOOK ME TO THE UNDERGROUND CHAMBER FULL OF LIGHT, I STILL COULDN'T MAKE OUT WHAT THEY WERE TRYING TO SHOW ME.
WHERE'S GRAN'MA BEN?
SHE WENT TO RESCUE PHONEY BONE AND DOESN'T HAVE ANY IDEA WHAT HAPPENED TO US.
OH, I REMEMBER.
WE WERE UP ON THE RAMPARTS LOOKING FOR - -
OHMYGOSH.
BRIAR AND THE RAT CREATURES! THEY'RE COMING TO ATTACK US!
WE HAVE TO GET OUT OF HERE AND HELP GRAN'MA BEN! SHE CAN'T DEFEND THE CITY BY HERSELF - -
WELL, IT'S A CINCH WE CAN'T DO A THING ABOUT IT FROM HERE.
HOW IRONIC THAT WE'RE TRYING TO SAVE THE CITY, AND THE CITY'S OWN SOLDIERS ARE TRYING TO STOP US!
HEY...
WHAT'S WRONG?
I THINK ONE OF MY TEETH IS - -
oh, No...

OH, FONE BONE.
WHAT ARE WE GOING TO DO?
DON'T WORRY, THORN, WE'LL GET OUT OF THIS OKAY - -

LOOK, LORD TARSIL! THEY ARE SENDING A DELEGATION!
HOLD YOUR GROUND...

HEY, YOU!
CLEAR THE RAMPARTS!
CAN'T YOU SEE WE'RE UNDER ATTACK? SEEK SHELTER WITH THE OTHER OLD WOMEN - -
WAIT! IT'S QUEEN ROSE!
YOUR MAJESTY! WE HEARD YOU WERE BACK IN THE CITY BUT WE DIDN'T DARE HOPE IT WAS TRUE!
I CAN SEE THERE'S NO EYE SYMBOL ON YOUR HOODS, BUT I DON'T HAVE TIME TO PLAY, BOYS . . . ARE YOU GOING TO ARREST ME OR NOT?

WE ARE NOT VEDU! WE HAVE NO LOYALTY TO THE TYRANT TARSIL.
OUR WEAPONS ARE YOURS, HIGHNESS. WE SERVE ONLY YOU.
SURRENDER, ATHEIA!
YOUR LONG REIGN AS MASTERS OF THE VALLEY HAS COME TO AN END...
WE OFFER YOU ONE CHANCE TO LIVE...
OPEN THE GATES AND SURRENDER... OPPOSE US AND DIE!

WHAT IS YOUR ANSWER?!
IF YOU WANT TO SERVE ME, DO IT NOW.
GET OUT YOUR TINDERBOXES AND STRIKE ME A FIRE.
WHY SHOULD WE ANSWER TO A MOB THAT GATHERS AT OUR DOORSTEP?
WHO DARES APPROACH THE WORLD'S MIGHTIEST CITADEL WITH A RAGTAG ARMY OF HILLPEOPLE?
I DO....
AND I HAVE A FAR GREATER CLAIM TO THIS CITY THAN YOU, O TARSIL THE USURPER....
I AM THE PRINCESS BRIAR.... AND I HAVE COME TO RECLAIM MY KINGDOM.

I WARN YOU FOR THE LAST TIME . . . LAY DOWN YOUR ARMS AND SURRENDER UNCONDITIONALLY.
THIS ARMY IS PROTECTED BY THE LORD OF THE LOCUST AND CANNOT BE DEFEATED . . .
YOUR FAMILY NO LONGER RULES HERE. TAKE YOUR BLACK ARMY AND LEAVE!
YOU DO NOT FRIGHTEN US WITH YOUR LITTLE SPELLS!
YES . . . I THOUGHT YOU WOULD SAY THAT . . . . I SEE THERE IS STILL MUCH TO TEACH YOU ABOUT FEAR . . . .
YOU CAN'T TEACH ME ANY-THING!
I HAVE FOUGHT WITH DRAGONS!

HEH
HEH
HEH
HA!
AH?
WHAT IS SHE DOING?
THAT'S TARSIL'S OLD FACE - -
HA! HA! HA!
AREN'T I HANDSOME?

HAHAHAHAHAHA

HEH HEH HEH..,

HEH HEH HEH HAHAHA!
ATTACK!
FOR THE GLORY OF THE LOCUST WHO SHIELDS YOU FROM HARM!
ATTACK!
ATTACK!
AAAAAAAAAHHHH
BAR THE GATE!
SET FIRE TO THOSE BUILDINGS NEAR THE WALL!

ARCHERS FORWARD! USE YOUR PIKES TO PUSH BACK THEIR LADDERS!

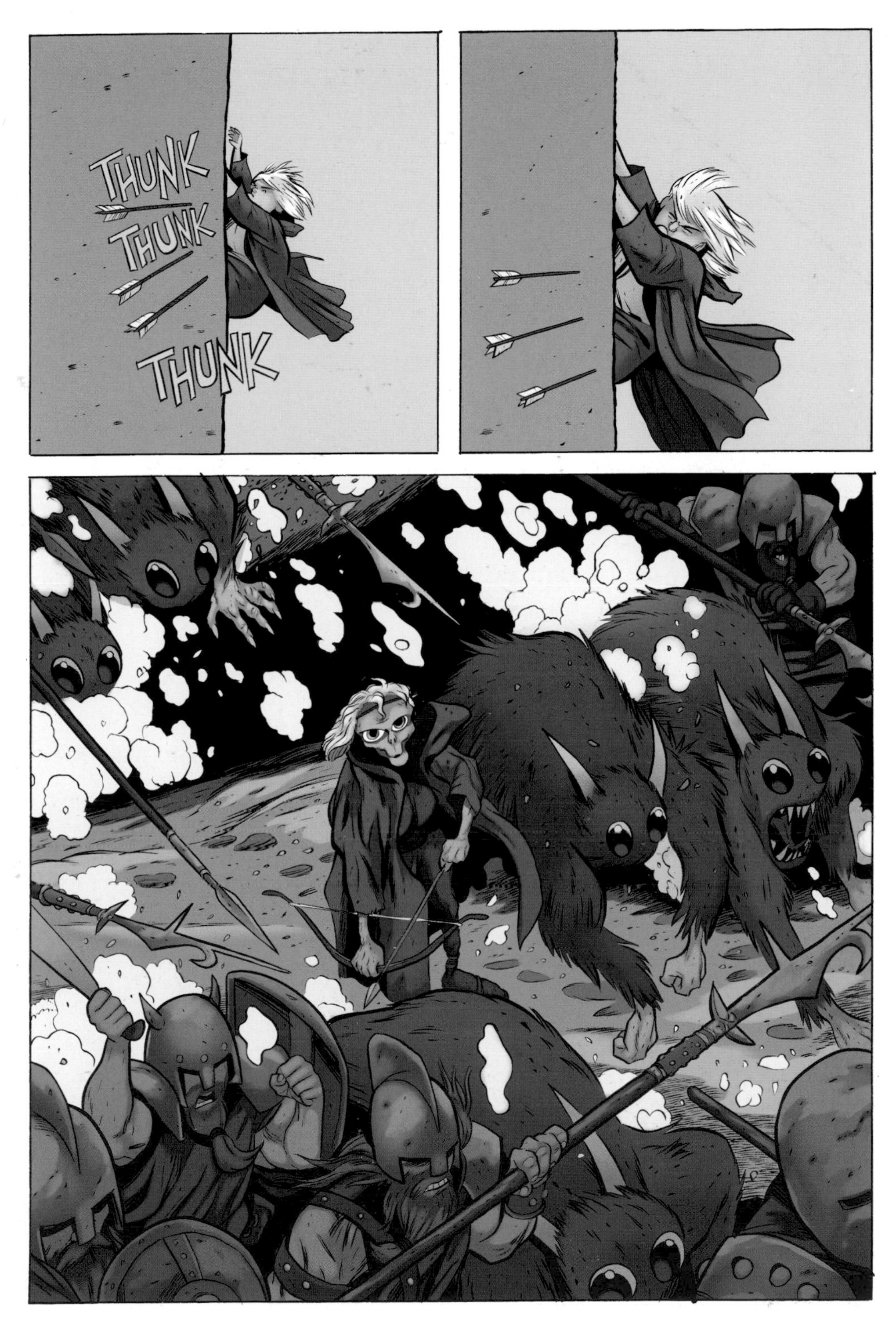
THUNK
THUNK
THUNK

DO YOU HEAR THAT?
I THINK THE WAR HAS STARTED...

HEY!
GUARD!
CAN ANYBODY HEAR ME?! WE HAVE TO GET OUT OF HERE!
WE HEAR YA, CUZ!
SMILEY?

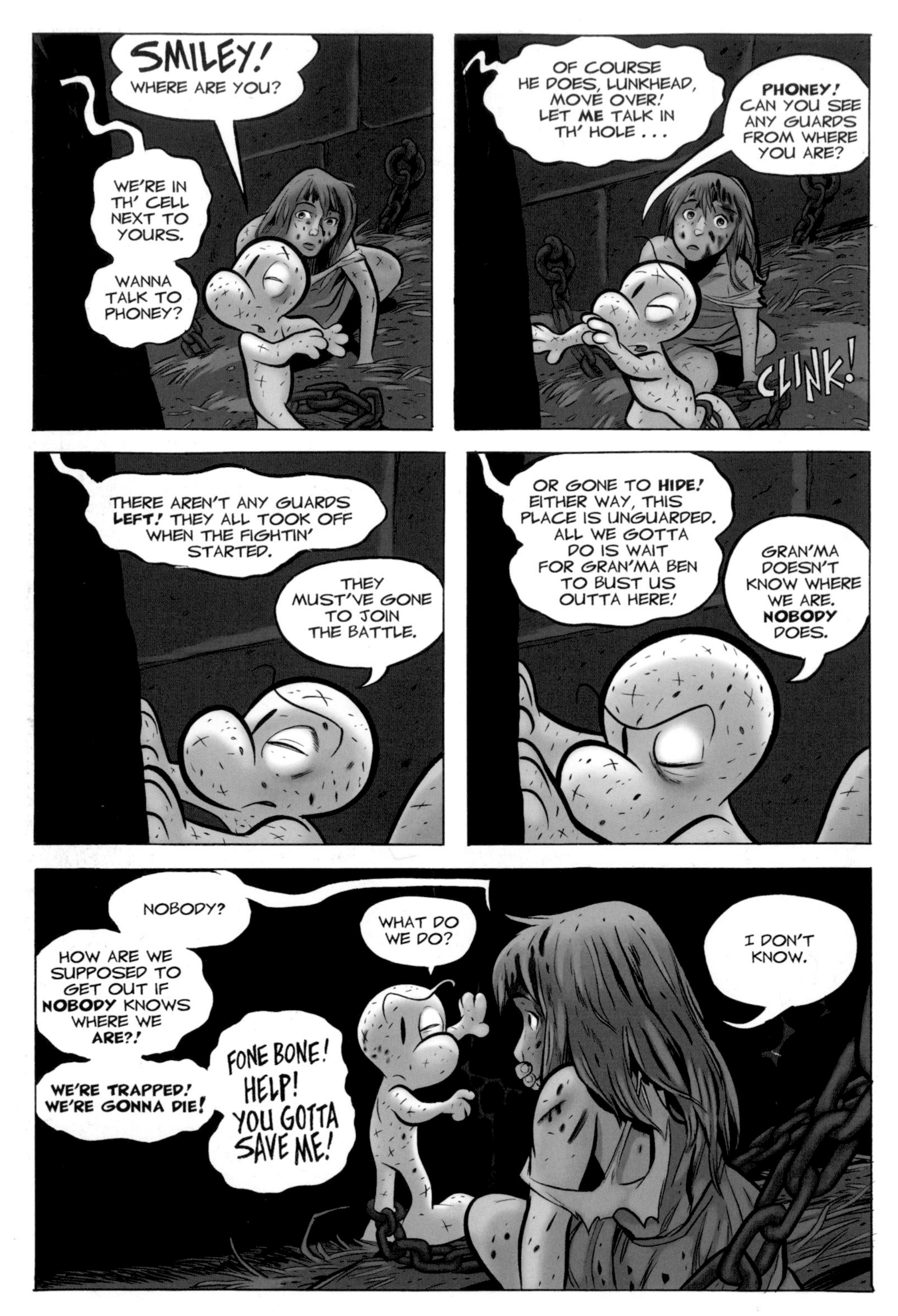
SMILEY! WHERE ARE YOU?
WE'RE IN TH' CELL NEXT TO YOURS.
WANNA TALK TO PHONEY?
OF COURSE HE DOES, LUNKHEAD, MOVE OVER! LET ME TALK IN TH' HOLE . . .
PHONEY! CAN YOU SEE ANY GUARDS FROM WHERE YOU ARE?
CLINK!
THERE AREN'T ANY GUARDS LEFT! THEY ALL TOOK OFF WHEN THE FIGHTIN' STARTED.
THEY MUST'VE GONE TO JOIN THE BATTLE.
OR GONE TO HIDE! EITHER WAY, THIS PLACE IS UNGUARDED. ALL WE GOTTA DO IS WAIT FOR GRAN'MA BEN TO BUST US OUTTA HERE!
GRAN'MA DOESN'T KNOW WHERE WE ARE. NOBODY DOES.
NOBODY?
HOW ARE WE SUPPOSED TO GET OUT IF NOBODY KNOWS WHERE WE ARE?!
WE'RE TRAPPED! WE'RE GONNA DIE!
FONE BONE! HELP! YOU GOTTA SAVE ME!
WHAT DO WE DO?
I DON'T KNOW.

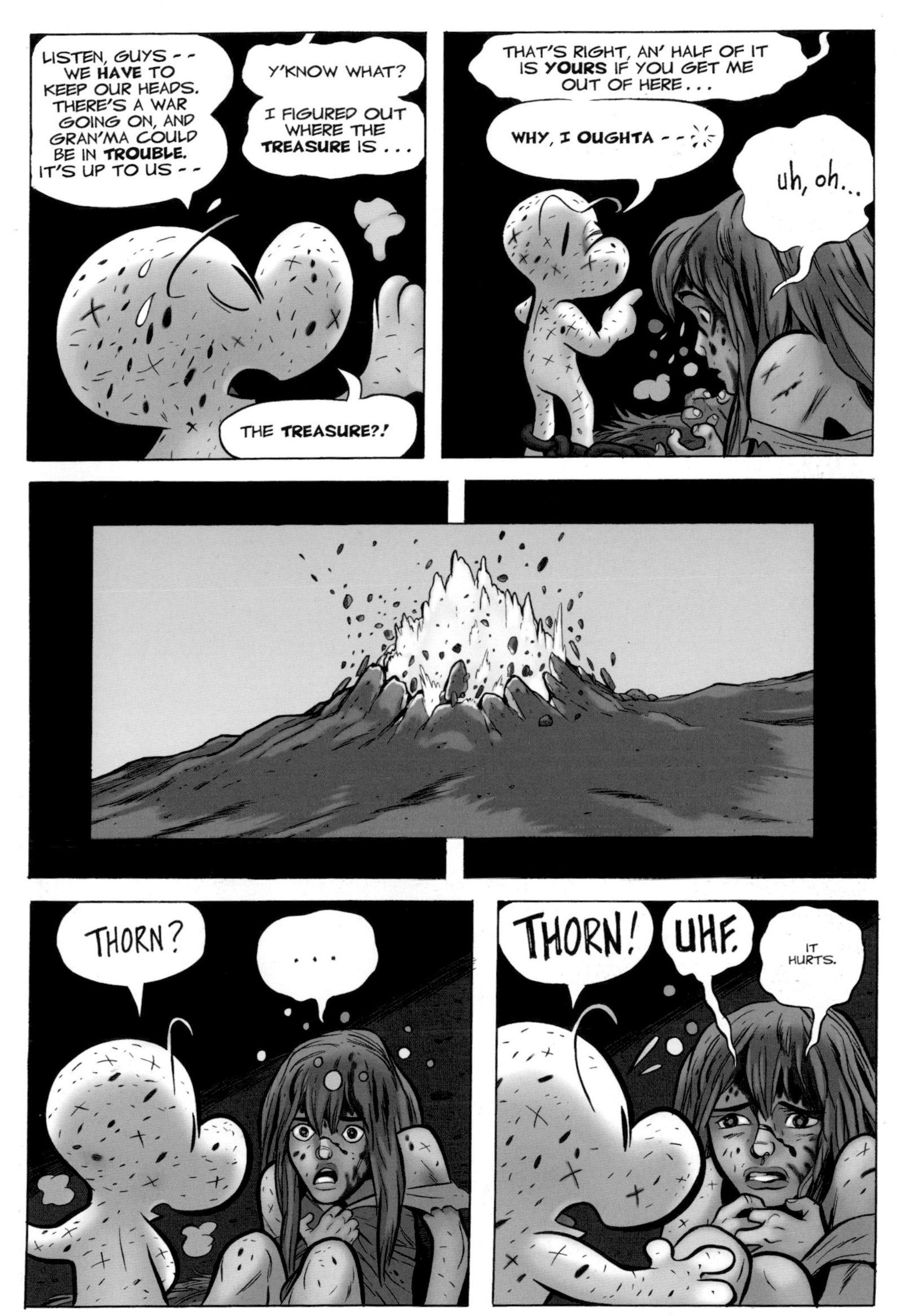
LISTEN, GUYS - - WE HAVE TO KEEP OUR HEADS. THERE'S A WAR GOING ON, AND GRAN'MA COULD BE IN TROUBLE. IT'S UP TO US - -
Y'KNOW WHAT?
I FIGURED OUT WHERE THE TREASURE IS . . .
THE TREASURE?!
THAT'S RIGHT, AN' HALF OF IT IS YOURS IF YOU GET ME OUT OF HERE . . .
WHY, I OUGHTA - -
uh, oh...
THORN?
. . .
THORN!
UHF.
IT HURTS.

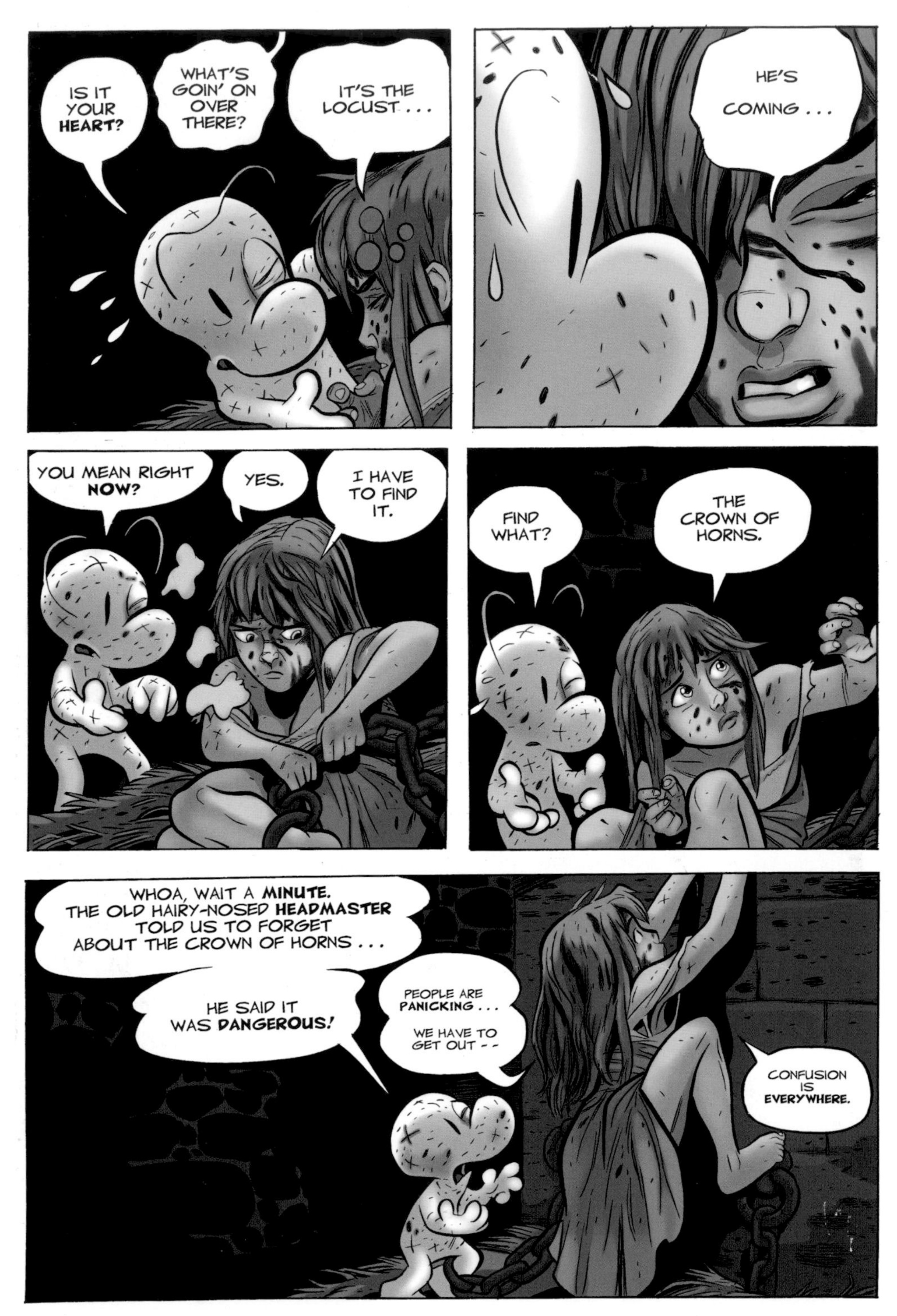
IS IT YOUR HEART?
WHAT'S GOIN' ON OVER THERE?
IT'S THE LOCUST . . .
HE'S COMING . . .
YOU MEAN RIGHT NOW?
YES.
I HAVE TO FIND IT.
FIND WHAT?
THE CROWN OF HORNS.
WHOA, WAIT A MINUTE. THE OLD HAIRY-NOSED HEADMASTER TOLD US TO FORGET ABOUT THE CROWN OF HORNS . . .
HE SAID IT WAS DANGEROUS!
PEOPLE ARE PANICKING . . .
WE HAVE TO GET OUT - -
CONFUSION IS EVERYWHERE.

AAAA!

YOUR MAJESTY!
HERE COMES ANOTHER ONE!
LOOK OUT!

WHAK!

MAJESTY!
THE ENEMY IS GATHERING FOR AN ATTACK ON OUR LEFT FLANK -- WHERE OUR FORCES ARE WEAKEST.
LET'S GO -- DO AS MUCH DAMAGE ON THE WAY AS POSSIBLE.
WHY ARE YOU STILL STANDING THERE? YOU HEARD THE QUEEN!
IS THE ORDER OF THE EYE WITH US OR AGAINST US?

DO NOT EXPECT US TO BOW DOWN TO YOUR EXILED QUEEN, BROTHER.
- - UNDER THE CIRCUMSTANCES - - WE ARE WITH YOU.
BUT EVEN WITH ALL THE DISCIPLES OF VENU FIGHTING AS ONE . . .
. . . I AM AFRAID THE ENEMY'S NUMBERS WILL OVERWHELM US.
HERE THEY COME!
STAY TOGETHER! DON'T LET THEM SEPARATE YOU!
AAAAH!
AAIEE- -
CHING
KASH!

CLANG!
AAAAAAAA
THERE'S TOO MANY!
AAAH!
IT'S THE QUEEN!
HA!
THAT'S IT - -
HOLD HER . . .

AH!
THORN! WHAT ARE YOU DOING?!
TRYING TO GET OUT.
RRR.
YOU KNOW I'D FOLLOW YOU ANYWHERE -- BUT THE CROWN OF HORNS IS OFF-LIMITS!
GRAB THIS CHAIN -- MAYBE WE CAN PULL IT LOOSE.
EENH!
WHEN YOU WRESTLED WITH THE LOCUST IN YOUR DREAMS, YOU WERE INFECTED...
IF YOU SO MUCH AS TOUCH THE CROWN OF HORNS, IT COULD SET OFF A CHAIN REACTION!
A CHAIN REACTION THAT WILL KILL EVERYTHING!
I DON'T BELIEVE THAT.
LET'S TRY AGAIN.
YOU DON'T?
MY MOTHER WOULDN'T HAVE TOLD ME TO FIND IT IF IT WAS GOING TO KILL EVERYTHING.

BUT YOU **DO** THINK THE CHAIN REACTION WILL KILL THE LOCUST, RIGHT. . . ?
WHAT ARE YOU GUYS TALKING ABOUT? WHAT KINDA CROWN?
IT'S A SACRED OBJECT THAT BELONGS TO THE DRAGONS. IF I CAN **FIND** IT, I CAN STOP THE WAR.
THORN . . . LISTEN.
YOU THINK IT **WILL** KILL THE LOCUST.
YES.
THAT MEANS IT WILL KILL YOU, TOO. THE LOCUST IS PART OF YOU NOW.
DOESN'T IT MEAN THAT?
HELP ME GET THIS SHACKLE OFF.
IT **DOES** MEAN THAT!
PROMISE ME YOU WON'T DO IT!

THORN!
THORN--
PROMISE ME PLEASE!
OKAY, I PROMISE.
GOOD.
LET'S GET OUT OF HERE.

HELLO!
MR. BONE! SISTER THORN!
IT'S TANEAL!
YES, HELLO! IT IS ME! DO YOU REMEMBER MY BROTHER? HE IS GETTING YOUR COUSINS OUT OF THE CELL NEXT TO YOURS!
HERE.
WHILE I WORK ON THE BARS UP HERE, YOU KNOCK THE CHAINS OFF.
WAIT!
DO NOT MAKE A SOUND!
SOMETHING IS HAPPENING ON THE FAR SIDE OF THE COURTYARD - - MANY SOLDIERS ARE GATHERING.
I MUST HIDE.
PLEASE . . . STAY QUIET UNTIL I COME BACK.

httt...
THORN!
SISTER THORN, WE ARE BACK . . .
FONE BONE! WE'RE OUT THANKS TO THESE TWO - -
HEY - - WHAT'S GOIN' ON DOWN THERE?
Erk
THORN'S NOT BREATHING!
QUICK, KID! GIMME TH' HAMMER!
SISTER, I OVERHEARD THE SOLDIERS BEFORE THEY RAN AWAY- - THEY SAID SOMETHING BAD HAD HAPPENED. . .
BAM!

BAM!
. . .TARSIL IS **DEAD.** KILLED BEFORE THE GATE IN FRONT OF HIS OWN PEOPLE.
AND YOUR GRANDMOTHER WAS SEEN FIGHTING NEARBY, BUT SHE WAS OVERWHELMED BY THE ENEMY WHO POURED OVER THE PARAPET!
AAAAAA!
WHICH WAY IS THE GATE?

CAN'T YOU HOLD HER?!
GET OUT OF THE WAY- -
I'LL CUT HER HEAD OFF!
LOOK OUT!
BLOODY STARS!

AAH!
RUN! WE CAN'T FIGHT THAT!
?
MERMIE?
NOTHING TO FEAR, YOUR HIGHNESS. JUST A SIMPLE VISION TO CHASE OFF OUR ENEMIES.
MERMIE! THANK GOODNESS! WHERE ARE THE OTHER DREAM MASTERS?
RIGHT BEHIND ME.
YOUR MAJESTY, THANK THE STARS YOU ARE SAFE!
TEACHER, WHERE IS MY GRAND-DAUGHTER?
WE THOUGHT SHE WAS WITH YOU - -

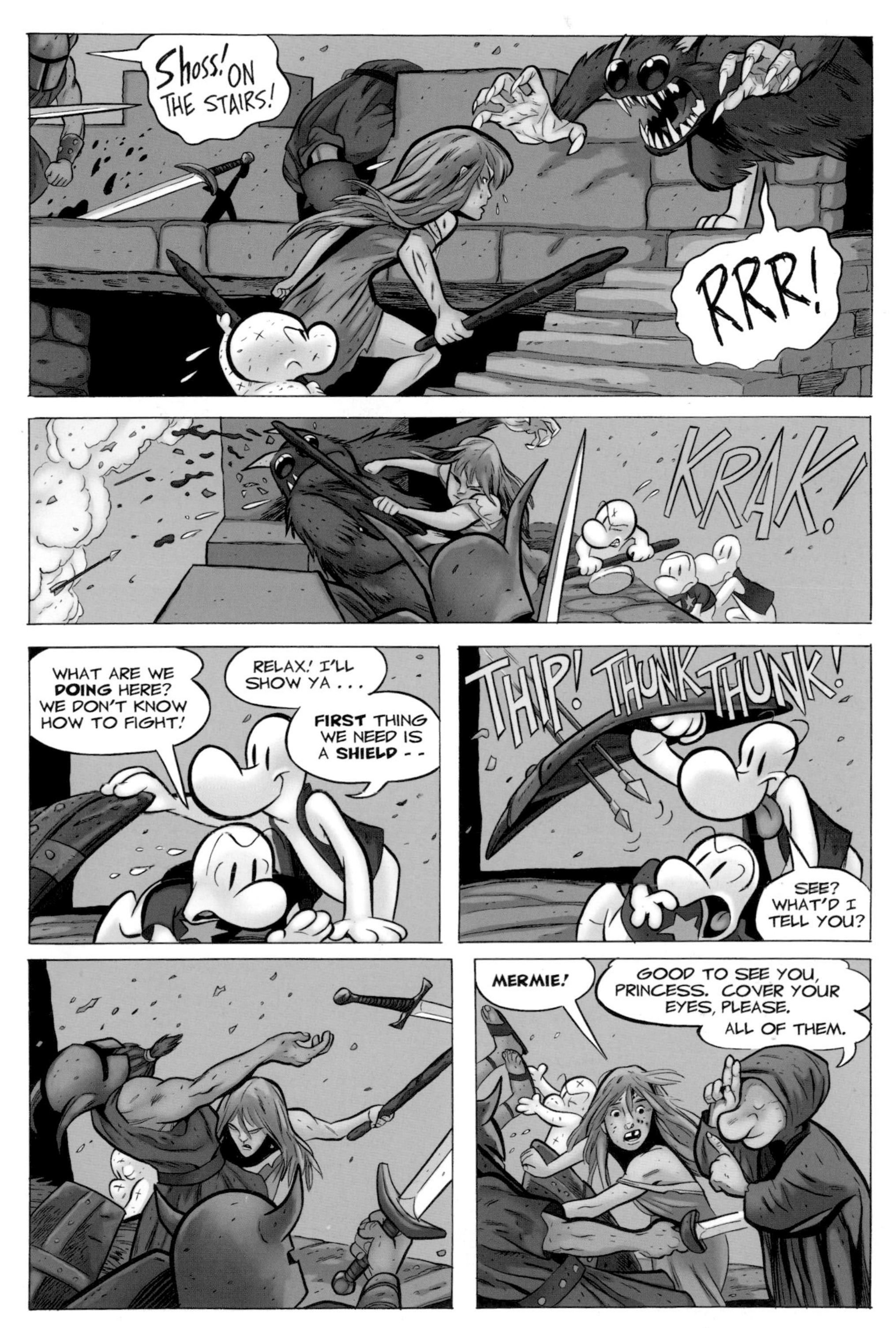
Shoss! ON THE STAIRS!
RRR!
KRAK!
WHAT ARE WE DOING HERE? WE DON'T KNOW HOW TO FIGHT!
RELAX! I'LL SHOW YA . . .
FIRST THING WE NEED IS A SHIELD - -
THIP! THUNK THUNK!
SEE? WHAT'D I TELL YOU?
MERMIE!
GOOD TO SEE YOU, PRINCESS. COVER YOUR EYES, PLEASE.
ALL OF THEM.

GRAN'MA!
THORN!
LET ME KISS YOUR FACE!
HEY! WE DID IT! THEY'RE RUNNING AWAY!

THE RAT CREATURES AND THE PAWANS ARE RETREATING!
TEACHER! YOUR DREAM-VISIONS FRIGHTENED OFF THE ENTIRE **INVASION FORCE!**
UNLIKELY.
EVEN POWERFUL VISIONS LIKE MERMIE'S CAN ONLY BE SEEN BY SMALL GROUPS AT A TIME.
THEN - -?
I DO NOT KNOW, BUT CLEARLY YOUR SISTER CALLED THEM BACK FOR A REASON.
WHY?
LOOK!

SOMETHING IS HAPPENING TO THE STARS . . .
THEY'RE TURNING **RED.**
WHAT IS IT, THORN? IT LOOKS LIKE THE STARS ARE GOING **OUT.**
THEY'RE ONLY GOING OUT FOR US.
GHOST CIRCLES ARE DESCENDING AROUND THE CITY.

BONE
LOOK AGAIN INTO THE LIGHT.
WHAT DO YOU SEE?
I --
IT IS TOO BRIGHT.
I'M SORRY...
WHEN THE WORLD WAS NEW, AND DREAMS HAD NOT YET RECEDED FROM THE WAKING DAY...
...DRAGONS RULED THE EARTH.

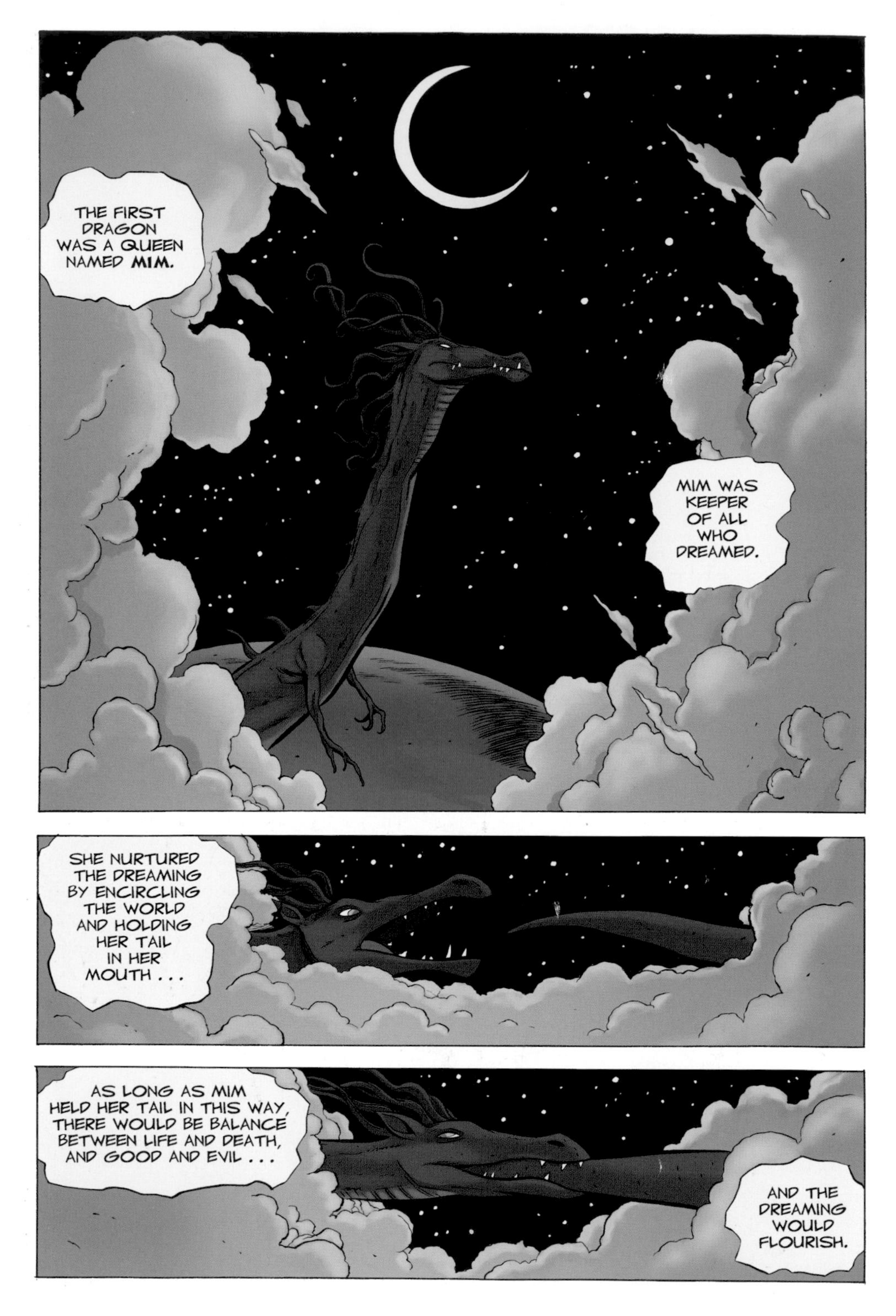
THE FIRST DRAGON WAS A QUEEN NAMED MIM.
MIM WAS KEEPER OF ALL WHO DREAMED.
SHE NURTURED THE DREAMING BY ENCIRCLING THE WORLD AND HOLDING HER TAIL IN HER MOUTH . . .
AS LONG AS MIM HELD HER TAIL IN THIS WAY, THERE WOULD BE BALANCE BETWEEN LIFE AND DEATH, AND GOOD AND EVIL . . .
AND THE DREAMING WOULD FLOURISH.

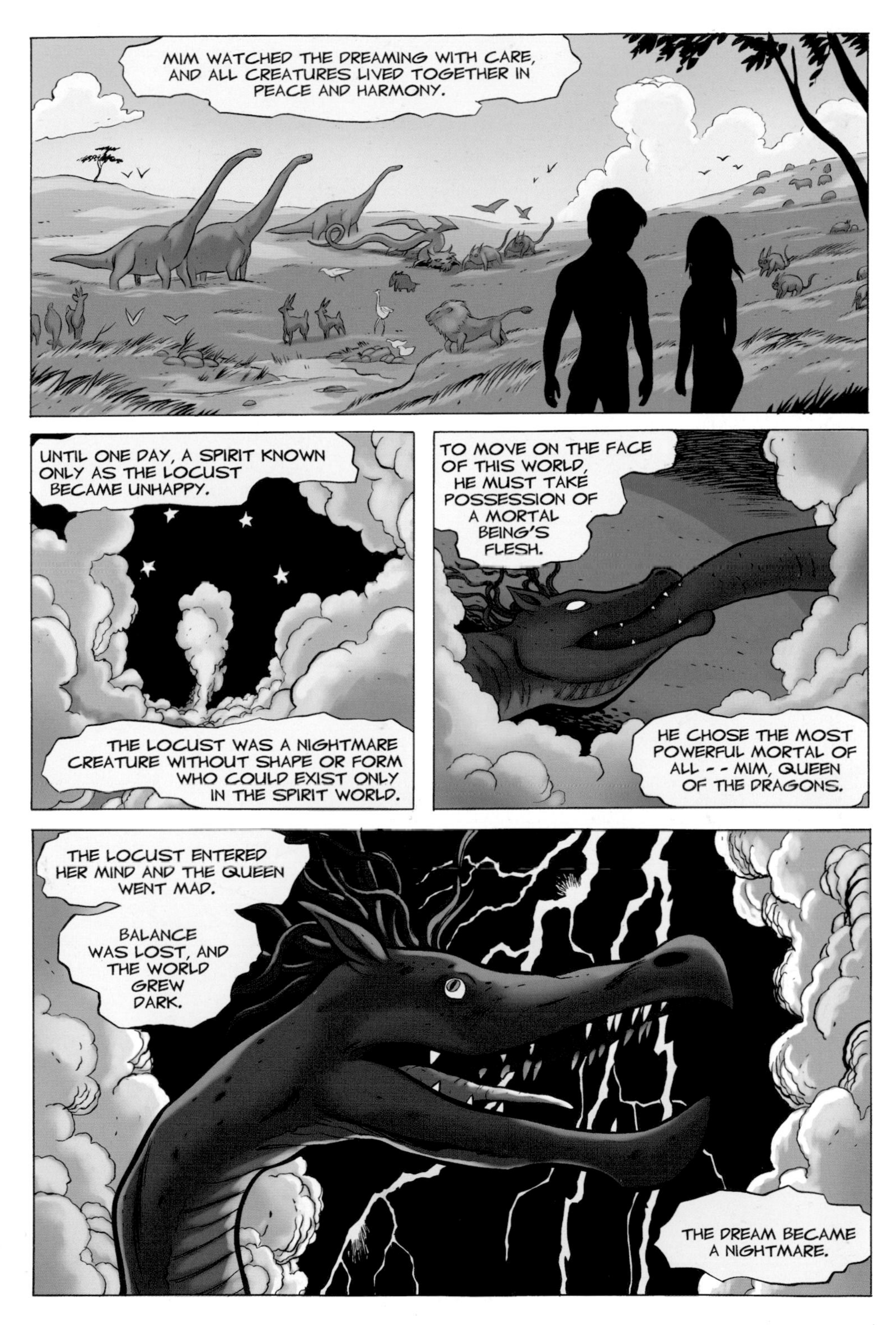
MIM WATCHED THE DREAMING WITH CARE, AND ALL CREATURES LIVED TOGETHER IN PEACE AND HARMONY.
UNTIL ONE DAY, A SPIRIT KNOWN ONLY AS THE LOCUST BECAME UNHAPPY.
THE LOCUST WAS A NIGHTMARE CREATURE WITHOUT SHAPE OR FORM WHO COULD EXIST ONLY IN THE SPIRIT WORLD.
TO MOVE ON THE FACE OF THIS WORLD, HE MUST TAKE POSSESSION OF A MORTAL BEING'S FLESH.
HE CHOSE THE MOST POWERFUL MORTAL OF ALL - - MIM, QUEEN OF THE DRAGONS.
THE LOCUST ENTERED HER MIND AND THE QUEEN WENT MAD.
BALANCE WAS LOST, AND THE WORLD GREW DARK.
THE DREAM BECAME A NIGHTMARE.

TO SAVE THE WORLD, THE OTHER DRAGONS WERE FORCED TO MOVE AGAINST HER.
A TERRIBLE BATTLE ENSUED.

AS THE DRAGONS FOUGHT, THEY CRASHED BACK AND FORTH PUSHING UP ROCKS AND MOUNTAINS.

ON AND ON THEY STRUGGLED, WITH MANY VALIANT DRAGONS LOSING THEIR LIVES . . .

UNTIL AT LAST THE DRAGONS DESPAIRED OF SAVING THEIR QUEEN, AND WERE FORCED TO TAKE DESPERATE MEASURES.

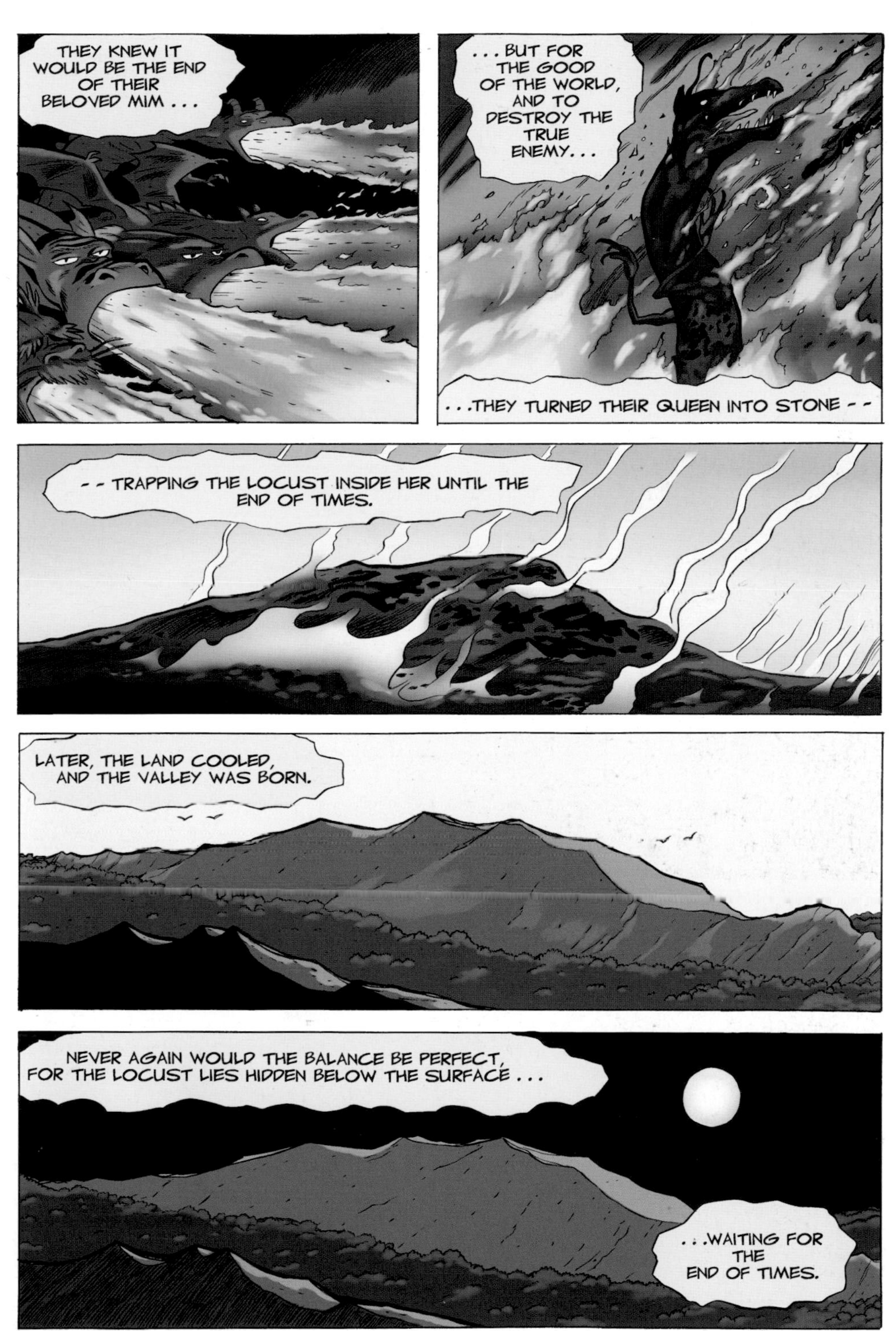
THEY KNEW IT WOULD BE THE END OF THEIR BELOVED MIM . . .
. . . BUT FOR THE GOOD OF THE WORLD, AND TO DESTROY THE TRUE ENEMY. . .
. . .THEY TURNED THEIR QUEEN INTO STONE - -
- - TRAPPING THE LOCUST INSIDE HER UNTIL THE END OF TIMES.
LATER, THE LAND COOLED, AND THE VALLEY WAS BORN.
NEVER AGAIN WOULD THE BALANCE BE PERFECT, FOR THE LOCUST LIES HIDDEN BELOW THE SURFACE . . .
. . .WAITING FOR THE END OF TIMES.

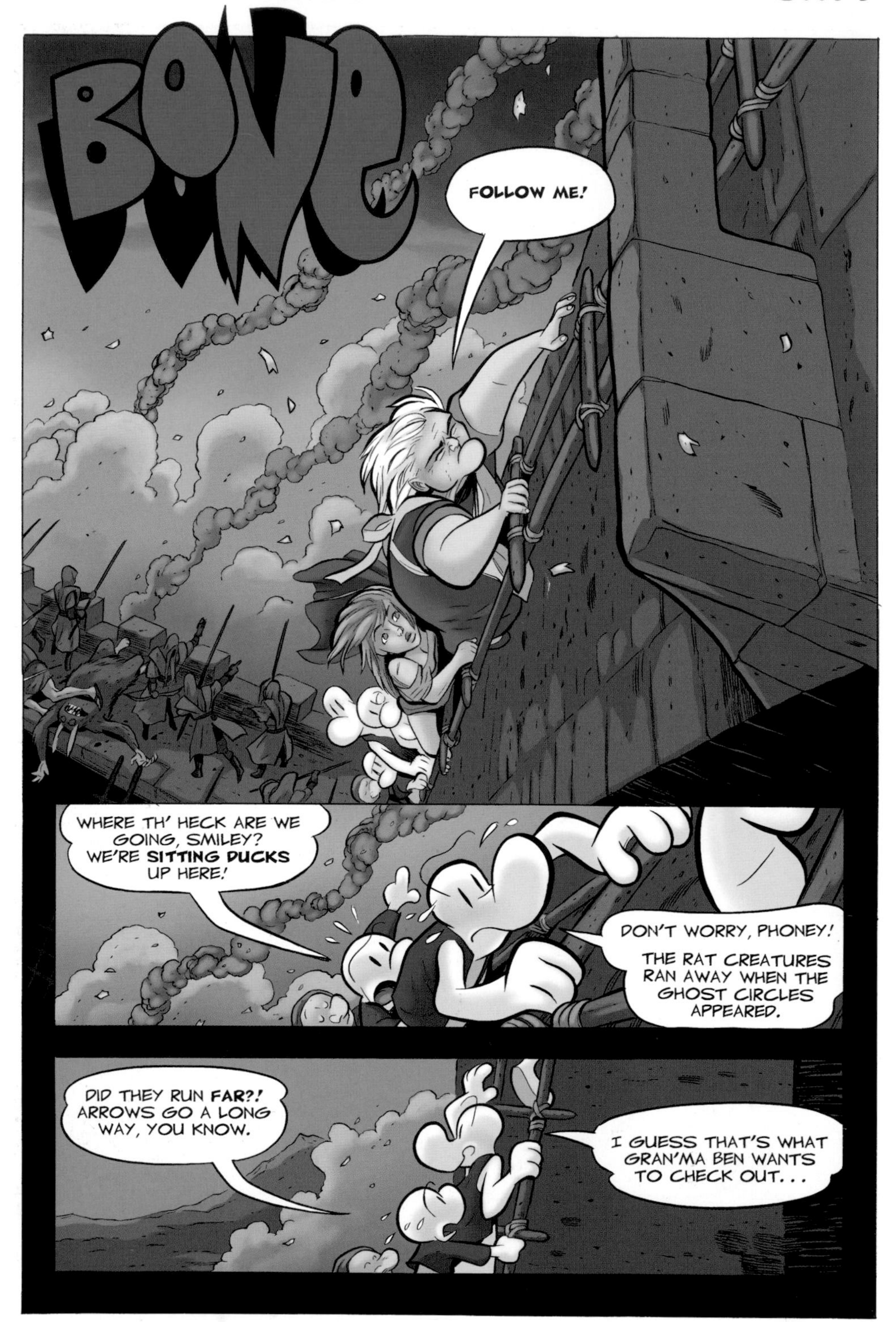
BONE
FOLLOW ME!
WHERE TH' HECK ARE WE GOING, SMILEY? WE'RE SITTING DUCKS UP HERE!
DON'T WORRY, PHONEY!
THE RAT CREATURES RAN AWAY WHEN THE GHOST CIRCLES APPEARED.
DID THEY RUN FAR?! ARROWS GO A LONG WAY, YOU KNOW.
I GUESS THAT'S WHAT GRAN'MA BEN WANTS TO CHECK OUT...

WHAT DO YOU SEE?

THE ENEMY HASN'T GONE AWAY. . . THEY'VE GATHERED INTO FOUR CAMPS.
WHAT ABOUT THE GHOST CIRCLES?
THEY RING THE CITY COMPLETELY. WE'RE SURROUNDED.

EVEN AROUND THE CLIFFS?
YES, AND THEY ARE VERY CLOSE...
OHMYGOSH, WE'RE TRAPPED! CAN THE GHOST CIRCLES HURT US?
THE GHOST CIRCLES CAN COME NO NEARER FOR THE MOMENT.
THERE IS TOO MUCH LIFE IN THIS CITY. PRINCESS BRIAR DOES NOT HAVE THE STRENGTH TO SNUFF IT OUT...
FOR THAT, SHE WILL NEED HER MASTER, THE LOCUST.
BRIAR MUST BE USING THE CIRCLES TO KEEP US FROM ESCAPING -- THE ONLY OPENINGS ARE DIRECTLY IN FRONT OF US.
WHERE?
THERE ARE FOUR GAPS. ONE FOR EACH ARMY...
THE FIRST IS IN THE WEST, UNDER SINNER'S ROCK. THE OTHER THREE ARE SPACED OUT ACROSS THE PLAIN TO THE EASTERN MOUNTAINS.

GAPS, EH? THAT'S INTERESTING...
THORN, LOOK PAST THE GHOST CIRCLES - -
IS ANYTHING ELSE OUT THERE?
WAIT- - YES!
THERE IS SOMETHING...
IT'S THAT GIANT MOUNTAIN LION!
ROCK JAW!
WHAT'S HE DOING SNEAKIN' AROUND HERE?
DON'T WE HAVE ENOUGH TROUBLE WITHOUT HIM STICKIN' HIS NOSE IN?!
HE'S UP IN THE EASTERN FOOTHILLS...
ALONE.
WE MAY NOT NEED TO WORRY- - ROQUE JA IS A MOUNTAIN CREATURE. I DON'T THINK HE'LL TAKE SIDES IN A VALLEY CONFLICT.
REALLY. HE ATTACKED YOU AND THORN - - SOUNDS LIKE HE PICKED SIDES TO ME.
HE'S ALSO A BIG CAT. YOU CAN'T ALWAYS EXPLAIN CATS.
THORN, PLEASE SEARCH BEYOND ROQUE JA... YOU KNOW WHAT I'M LOOKING FOR.

I'M SORRY, GRAN'MA. THERE'S NO SIGN OF LUCIUS OR THE WARRIORS FROM OLD MAN'S CAVE.
THERE ARE TOO MANY GHOST CIRCLES TO SEE IN THAT DIRECTION - -
BLOODY STARS.
I'M SORRY.
IT'S NOT YOUR FAULT, DEAR. IT'S MINE.
MY SISTER IS DETERMINED TO DESTROY EVERYONE I LOVE. ESPECIALLY LUCIUS.
AND I CAN'T STOP HER! DEATH CAN'T STOP HER - -
WHAT DO YOU WANT, BRIAR?!
YOU WANT ME? IF I COME OUT THERE, WILL YOU LEAVE EVERYONE ELSE ALONE?!
TAKE IT EASY, GRAN'MA! YOU CAN'T BLAME YOURSELF FOR WHO YOU'RE RELATED TO!
YEAH, LOOK AT US!
DON'T WORRY, GRAN'MA. LUCIUS WILL BE OKAY.
YOUR HIGHNESS! I'VE JUST HAD A TROUBLING THOUGHT.
YOUR SISTER COULD BE TRYING TO USE THE GHOST CIRCLES TO CREATE FEAR.
FEAR WEAKENS THE SPIRIT, WHICH IS OUR ONLY COUNTERBALANCE AGAINST THE GREAT EMPTINESS OF THE HOUSE OF MIST.
IF THE BALANCE EVER TIPPED TOO FAR - -

CHUNKRRRRUMMMBLLE...
LOOK OUT!
HHG!
THORN?!
NO-- I'M OKAY--
THORN, CAN YOU HEAR ME?!

Koff
Koff
IS EVERYONE ALL RIGHT?
WE'RE LUCKY THE WALLS DIDN'T COLLAPSE!
THERE'S SOMETHING WRONG WITH THORN!
. . .
ANYONE HURT UP HERE?
IT'S MY GRANDDAUGHTER! WE NEED TO GET HER DOWN TO THE ARMORY!
I HAVE HERBS.
YOUR MAJESTY, THE VEDU HAVE TAKEN OVER THE ARMORY AND WON'T LET ANYONE IN.
WHAT?! I THOUGHT THE VEDU WERE ON OUR SIDE!
GRAN'MA - -
NOW THAT YOU ARE IN CHARGE, THEY ARE AFRAID THEY WILL LOSE THEIR PRIVILEGES - -
THEY'RE NEGOTIATING?!
SOMETHING'S HAPPENING - -
UNDER TARSIL THE VEDU HAD MANY PRIVILEGES, AMONG THEM BONUS WAGES DURING BATTLE - -
PROMISE THEM ANYTHING! WE NEED TO GET IN THE ARMORY NOW!

WE'VE TRIED, BUT THEY DO NOT BELIEVE YOU --
TARSIL HID THE TREASURE AND TOOK THE SECRET TO HIS GRAVE --
WITHOUT THE TREASURE, YOU CAN'T BACK YOUR PROMISES --
RRR
HANG ON! IT'S AN AFTERSHOCK!
THORN!
RRR
GET THOSE VEDU OUT OR THEY'LL DEAL WITH ME!!
FONE BONE! I'VE GOT A PLAN!

SMILEY AN' I KNOW WHERE THE TREASURE IS . . . ALL WE HAVE TO DO IS LOAD IT ON A CART AND SNEAK IT OUT THROUGH ONE OF THE GAPS IN THE GHOST CIRCLES!
WHAT? ARE YOU TALKING TO ME?
YEAH, CUZ! THIS IS IT! WE'RE GOIN' HOME!
WHAT PLANET ARE YOU ON, PHONEY? WE'RE NOT GOING ANYWHERE!
OH, RIGHT! GOTCHA!
OKAY, WE'LL GET THE TREASURE . . . YOU MEET US AT THE MAIN GATE IN THIRTY MINUTES!
GET OUT OF HERE!
C'MON, SMILEY! HE'S GONNA MEET US AT THE GATE!
HIGHNESS?
MERMIE IS QUITE CONCERNED ABOUT THE AMOUNT OF FEAR THAT IS BEING RAISED AMONG OUR PEOPLE.
WHAT DO YOU EXPECT FROM THEM? THE CITY'S IN FLAMES - -
TERROR WEAKENS OUR SPIRIT, TIPPING THE BALANCE IN THE ENEMY'S FAVOR.
YOUR SISTER IS USING THE GHOST CIRCLES TO FORCE A BREACH IN THE DREAMING - -
THE LOCUST COULD ESCAPE.
IF WE DO NOT RESTORE ORDER IMMEDIATELY, THE LOCUST WILL GET OUT AND SEEK THE MORTAL FLESH OF A NEW HOST!
IT'S TOO LATE.

WHAT IF THE TREASURE ISN'T IN THE WELL?
OF COURSE IT'S IN THE WELL!
WHY ELSE WOULD TARSIL MAKE UP THAT STORY ABOUT THE POISONED GROUND WATER? HE WAS TRYIN' TO SCARE PEOPLE!
SCARE 'EM AWAY FROM THE TREASURE, HUH?
EXACTLY. NOW WE DON'T HAVE MUCH TIME -- YOU GO TO THE BARN AND GET THE HAY CART, THEN MEET ME BACK HERE!
CAN I BRING BARTLEBY WITH US?
NO! HE'S A RAT CREATURE!
BUT HE'S ONLY A BABY!
OKAY! OKAY! BRING HIM! JUST GET TH' CART!
WE'RE IN A HURRY!!

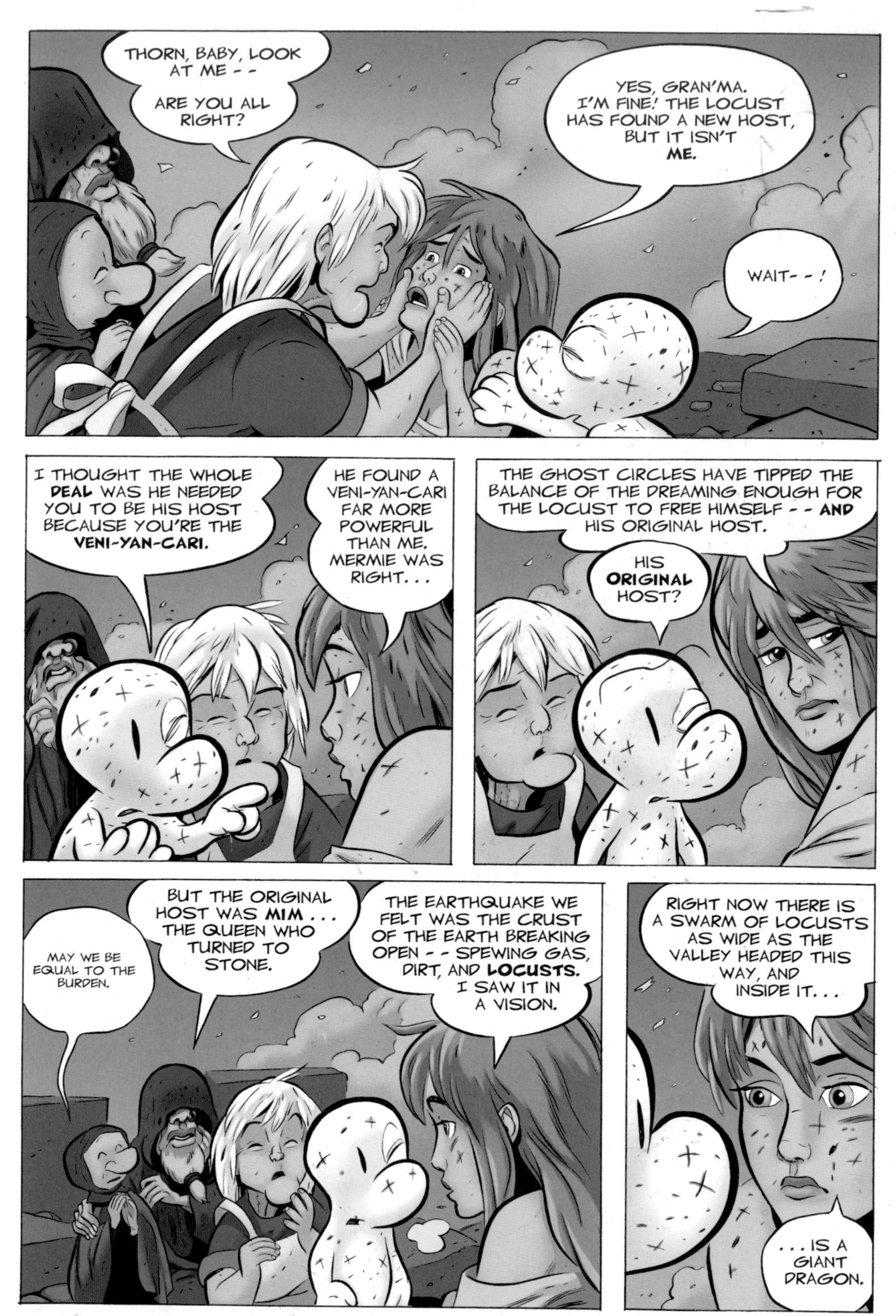
THORN, BABY, LOOK AT ME - -
ARE YOU ALL RIGHT?
YES, GRAN'MA. I'M FINE! THE LOCUST HAS FOUND A NEW HOST, BUT IT ISN'T **ME.**
WAIT- - !
I THOUGHT THE WHOLE **DEAL** WAS HE NEEDED YOU TO BE HIS HOST BECAUSE YOU'RE THE **VENI-YAN-CARI.**
HE FOUND A VENI-YAN-CARI FAR MORE POWERFUL THAN ME. MERMIE WAS RIGHT. . .
THE GHOST CIRCLES HAVE TIPPED THE BALANCE OF THE DREAMING ENOUGH FOR THE LOCUST TO FREE HIMSELF - - **AND** HIS ORIGINAL HOST.
HIS **ORIGINAL** HOST?
BUT THE ORIGINAL HOST WAS **MIM** . . . THE QUEEN WHO TURNED TO STONE.
MAY WE BE EQUAL TO THE BURDEN.
THE EARTHQUAKE WE FELT WAS THE CRUST OF THE EARTH BREAKING OPEN - - SPEWING GAS, DIRT, AND **LOCUSTS.** I SAW IT IN A VISION.
RIGHT NOW THERE IS A SWARM OF LOCUSTS AS WIDE AS THE VALLEY HEADED THIS WAY, AND INSIDE IT. . .
. . . IS A GIANT DRAGON.

IT IS MIM.
SHE'S STILL ALIVE. THAT'S WHY THE DRAGONS LEFT US - - THEY DON'T WANT TO FACE THEIR QUEEN.
YOUR MAJESTY- - IF IT IS MIM, AND SHE IS UNDER THE LOCUST'S SPELL, EVERYTHING IN HER PATH WILL BE DESTROYED!
LUCIUS.
US!

PHONEY! I'M BACK!
GOOD! GRAB THAT CHAIN AN' PULL IT UP!
NEED SOME HELP?
NO, BARTLEBY! NOW GET BACK IN THERE. WE'RE NOT TAKING ANY CHANCES ON YOU BEING SEEN!
HOW MUCH IS DOWN THERE?
PLENTY! GET A HAMMER AN' OPEN ONE UP!
WHAT DO YOU THINK IT WILL BE? GOLD? JEWELS?
YES! YES! ALL OF IT!
WHOO HOO! JACKPOT!
I KNEW IT!

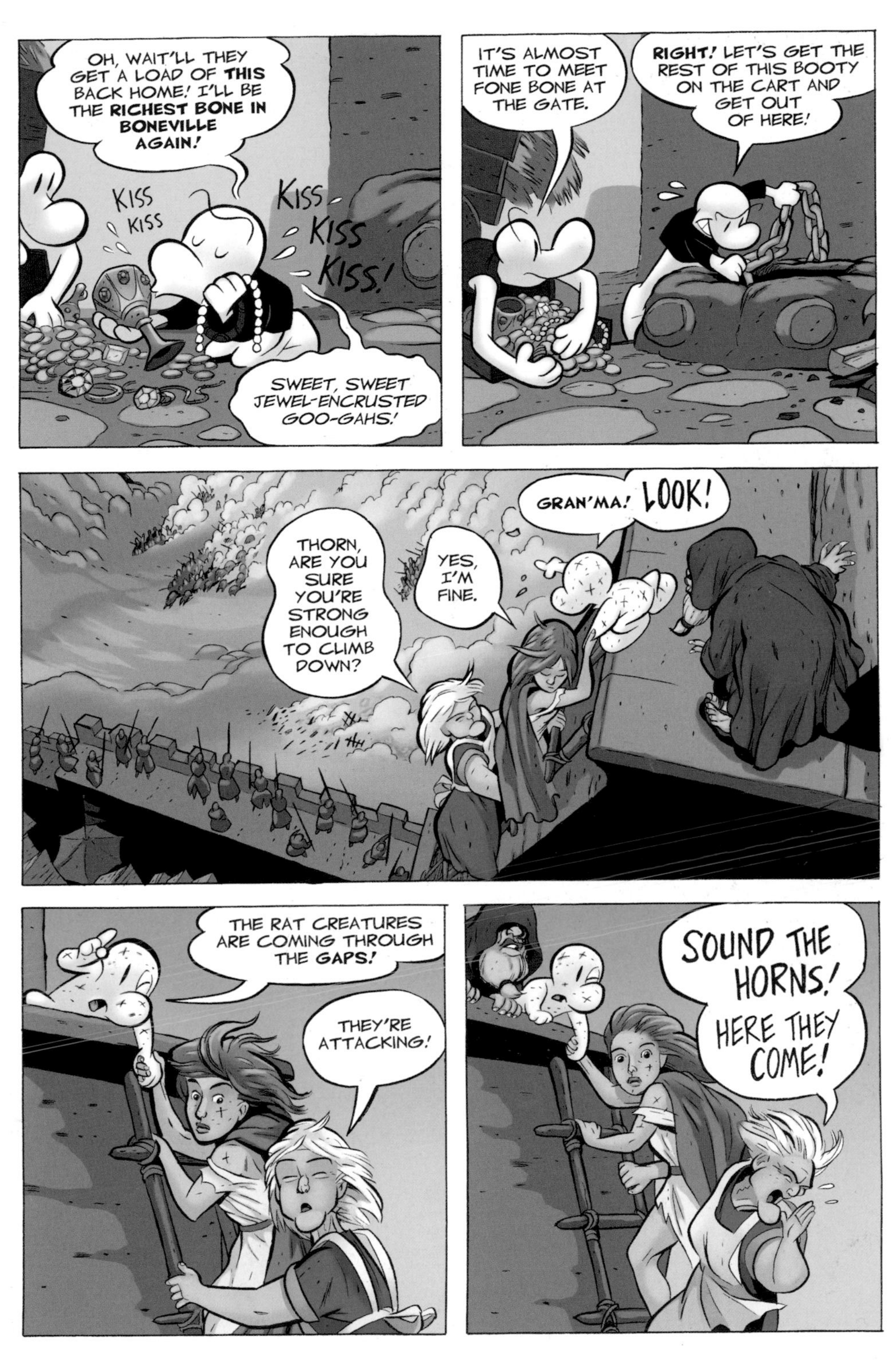
OH, WAIT'LL THEY GET A LOAD OF THIS BACK HOME! I'LL BE THE RICHEST BONE IN BONEVILLE AGAIN!
KISS KISS
KISS KISS KISS!
SWEET, SWEET JEWEL-ENCRUSTED GOO-GAHS!
IT'S ALMOST TIME TO MEET FONE BONE AT THE GATE.
RIGHT! LET'S GET THE REST OF THIS BOOTY ON THE CART AND GET OUT OF HERE!
GRAN'MA! LOOK!
THORN, ARE YOU SURE YOU'RE STRONG ENOUGH TO CLIMB DOWN?
YES, I'M FINE.
THE RAT CREATURES ARE COMING THROUGH THE GAPS!
THEY'RE ATTACKING!
SOUND THE HORNS! HERE THEY COME!

AWWOOOOOOAH!
AAWOOOOOAH!
EEEE!
ARE YOU SURE THIS IS GONNA WORK? WHAT IF FONE BONE DOESN'T MEET US AT THE GATE?
HE HAS TO. WHEN WE WERE IN THE GHOST CIRCLES HE SWORE A SOLEMN OATH TO ME HE'D LEAVE WHENEVER I SAID.
AAH! THE RAT CREATURES ARE COMING!
RUN!
EEE EEEE
WHAT IF THEY WON'T OPEN THE GATE FOR US?
SEE THIS LITTLE BEAUTY? WE'LL BUY OUR WAY OUT. RELAX! WE'RE PRACTICALLY HOME FREE!

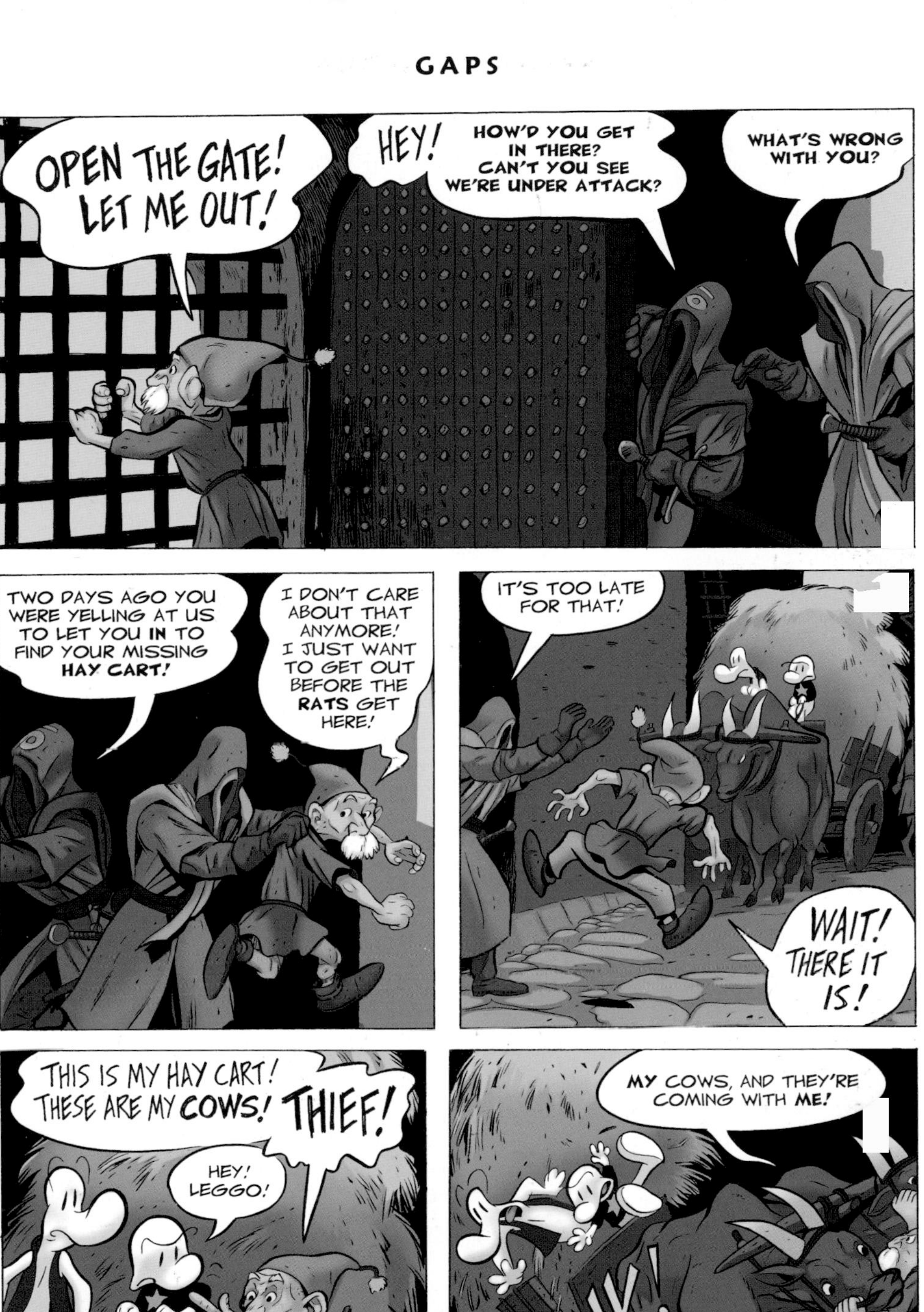
OPEN THE GATE! LET ME OUT!
HEY!
HOW'D YOU GET IN THERE? CAN'T YOU SEE WE'RE UNDER ATTACK?
WHAT'S WRONG WITH YOU?
TWO DAYS AGO YOU WERE YELLING AT US TO LET YOU IN TO FIND YOUR MISSING HAY CART!
I DON'T CARE ABOUT THAT ANYMORE! I JUST WANT TO GET OUT BEFORE THE RATS GET HERE!
IT'S TOO LATE FOR THAT!
WAIT! THERE IT IS!
THIS IS MY HAY CART! THESE ARE MY COWS!
THIEF!
HEY! LEGGO!
MY COWS, AND THEY'RE COMING WITH ME!
CRANK!

SPLAT!
HEY!
WHAT'S ALL THIS?!
CLEAR THIS MESS OUT!
ARREST THESE TWO!
I'LL ARREST YOU, IF YOU DON'T WATCH IT, TROUBLEMAKER!
EEEEEK! A RAT CREATURE!
THERE!
IT'S BARTLEBY!
HOW DID IT GET INSIDE THE WALLS?
WHERE IS IT?
DON'T LET IT GET AWAY!
BARTLEBY!
LOOK OUT!

HE'S CORNERED!
WATCH THAT SIDE - -
I'LL KILL IT!
RUN, BARTLEBY!
MY TREASURE - -
MY TREASURE . . .
PHONEY! HELP!
HELP US!
HERE!
OH, NO YOU DON'T! YOU'RE NOT HELPING THEM ESCAPE!
BAM!

NO!
LEAVE ME!
AAH!

GO THAT WAY!
LOOK! A RAT CREATURE!

THUNK! THUNK!

GRAN'MA! HELP!
WHAT?
LOOK OUT!
AN ANGRY MOB IS AFTER BARTLEBY!
I'LL HANDLE THIS.
UP YOU GO . . . QUICKLY.
EXCUSE ME, THORN . . . SORRY!
GO BACK UP!
HI, GUYS!
WHERE ARE YOU GOING? WE'RE COMIN' DOWN!
GET THE RAT CREATURE!
THERE HE IS - - ON THE LADDER!
HOLD IT! DON'T SHOOT!
- - I HAD NO CHOICE! PHONEY WANTS TO GO HOME, AND I CAN'T LEAVE BARTLEBY!
I SHOULD HAVE KNOWN THIS WAS PHONEY'S FAULT.

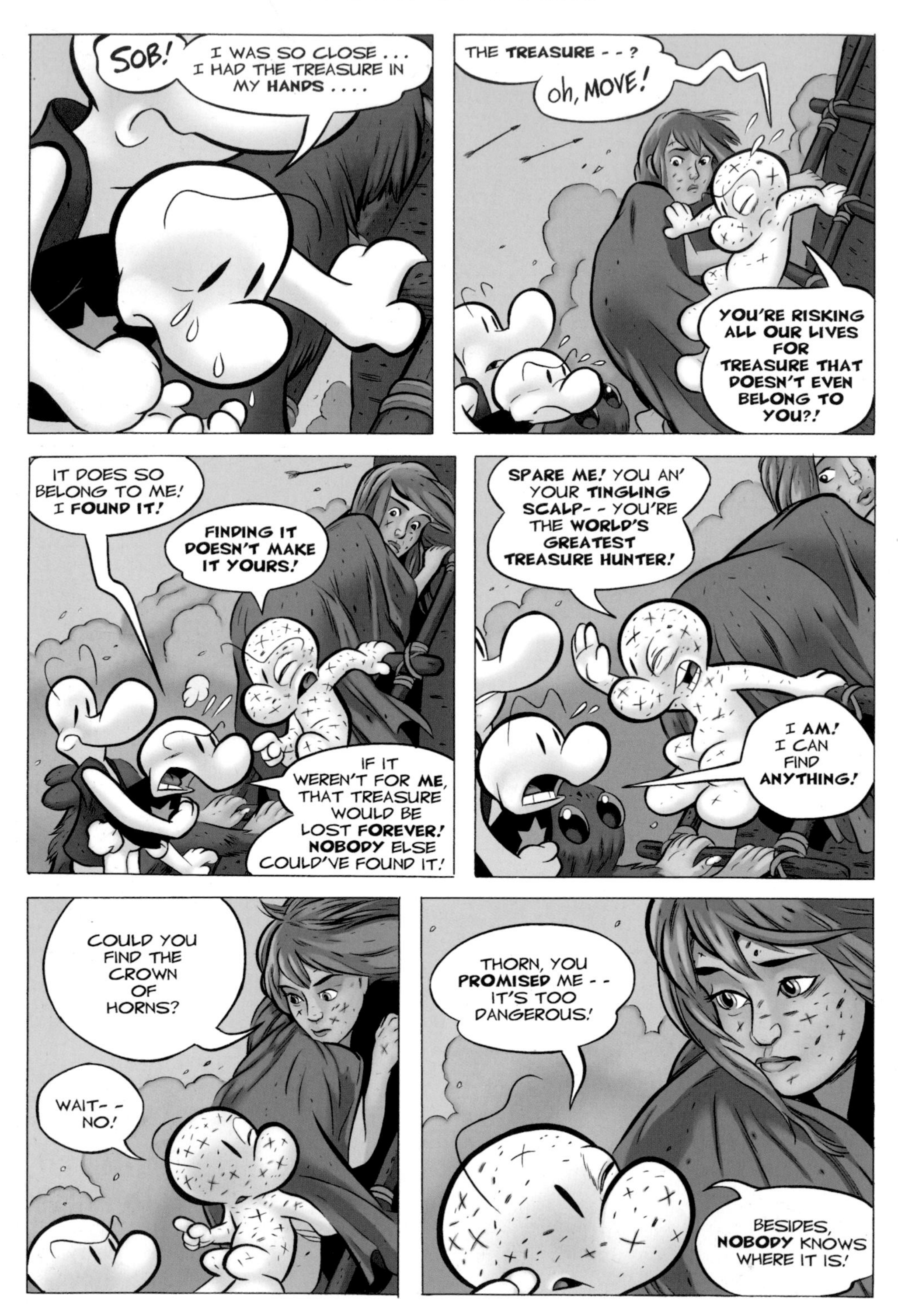
SOB!
I WAS SO CLOSE . . . I HAD THE TREASURE IN MY HANDS . . . .
THE TREASURE - - ?
oh, MOVE!
YOU'RE RISKING ALL OUR LIVES FOR TREASURE THAT DOESN'T EVEN BELONG TO YOU?!
IT DOES SO BELONG TO ME! I FOUND IT!
FINDING IT DOESN'T MAKE IT YOURS!
IF IT WEREN'T FOR ME, THAT TREASURE WOULD BE LOST FOREVER! NOBODY ELSE COULD'VE FOUND IT!
SPARE ME! YOU AN' YOUR TINGLING SCALP- - YOU'RE THE WORLD'S GREATEST TREASURE HUNTER!
I AM! I CAN FIND ANYTHING!
COULD YOU FIND THE CROWN OF HORNS?
WAIT- - NO!
THORN, YOU PROMISED ME - - IT'S TOO DANGEROUS!
BESIDES, NOBODY KNOWS WHERE IT IS!

I DO.
IT'S HIDDEN IN THE SACRED BURIAL GROUNDS OF THE DRAGONS.
OBVIOUSLY.
WHAT?
SURE! HAS TO BE. WHY ELSE WOULD THE DRAGONS WORK SO HARD TO SCARE EVERYBODY AWAY FROM THERE?
IT'S JUST LIKE TARSIL HIDIN' THE TREASURE IN THE WELL.
IT MATCHES MY DREAM! THE CROWN OF HORNS IS IN THE SACRED BURIAL GROUNDS IN TANEN GARD!
GREAT! THANK YOU! NOW SHE'S GONNA TRY AN' GO THERE!!
SO LET HER! WE'RE LEAVING FOR BONEVILLE ANYWAY!
I AM NOT LEAVING FOR BONEVILLE!!
YOU PROMISED ME!
WELL, I CAN'T KEEP THAT PROMISE!
AAAH!

THORN!
MERMIE! WHICH WAY DID THORN GO?
THORN! WAIT!
SHE JUMPED!
RIGHT INTO THE BURNING TOWN! SHE JUMPED!!
I CAN'T JUMP THAT FAR!
I CAN JUMP THAT FAR! CLIMB ON MY BACK, I'LL TAKE YOU TO HER!
HEY!

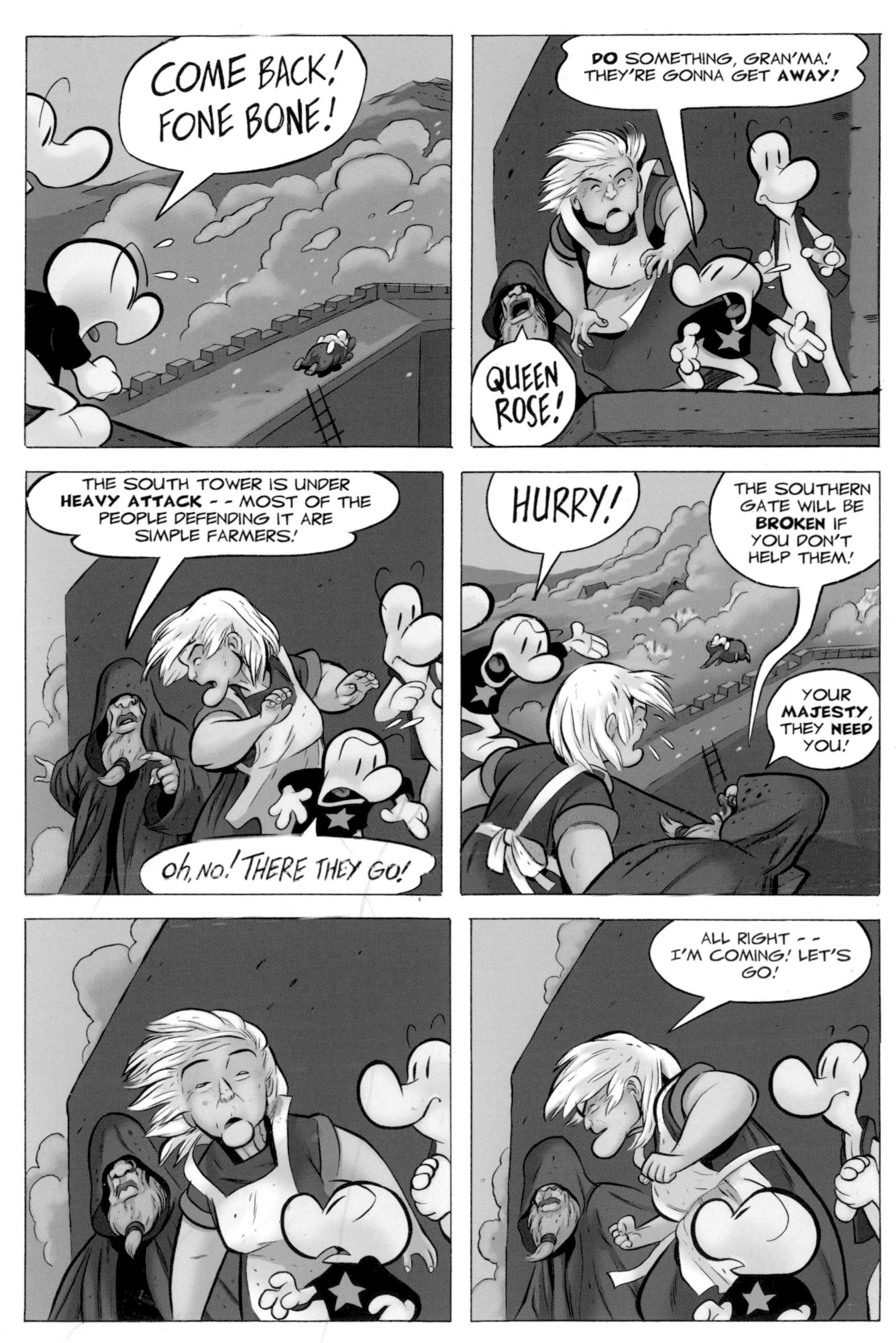
COME BACK! FONE BONE!
DO SOMETHING, GRAN'MA! THEY'RE GONNA GET AWAY!
QUEEN ROSE!
THE SOUTH TOWER IS UNDER HEAVY ATTACK - - MOST OF THE PEOPLE DEFENDING IT ARE SIMPLE FARMERS!
OH, NO! THERE THEY GO!
HURRY!
THE SOUTHERN GATE WILL BE BROKEN IF YOU DON'T HELP THEM!
YOUR MAJESTY, THEY NEED YOU!
ALL RIGHT - - I'M COMING! LET'S GO!

BONE
THORN! WHERE ARE YOU?
DON'T WORRY, FONE BONE. WE'LL FIND HER.
SHE HAS TO BE SOMEWHERE IN THE VILLAGE. SHE CAN'T GET PAST THE GHOST CIRCLES, RIGHT?
YEAH, YOU'RE RIGHT. THE RAT CREATURES CONTROL ALL THE GAPS IN THE BARRIER. ESCAPE'S IMPOSSIBLE.
SO WE BETTER BE CAREFUL - - IF WE STEP IN THE WRONG PLACE WE'LL DISAPPEAR IN A PUFF OF SMOKE!
THERE SHE IS!

SHE'S PICKING UP A SWORD FROM THAT DEAD GUY. HURRY, BARTLEBY, LET'S CATCH UP TO HER - -
WAIT! SOLDIERS ARE COMING!
HALT!
SKRAK
FFTZZ!
OH, NO!
DID YOU SEE THAT?! THORN RAN INTO A GHOST CIRCLE!
WE HAVE TO TAKE COVER!
SPREAD OUT AND SEARCH THE AREA! THERE COULD BE MORE SURVIVORS!

DO YOU THINK THORN IS ALIVE?
I DON'T KNOW. SHE MIGHT BE ABLE TO SURVIVE IN A GHOST CIRCLE . . .
SHE DID IT BEFORE.
MAYBE SHE IS ALIVE AND SHE'S GOING THROUGH THE GHOST CIRCLE TO ESCAPE THE CITY!
fft!
ZZK
YOU IDIOTS! I WARNED YOU TO BE CAREFUL!
NOW GET BACK TO CAMP BEFORE YOU ALL GET EVAPORATED!
HEY! THOSE RATS HAVE TO GO THROUGH ONE OF THE GAPS TO REACH THEIR CAMP.
COME ON! I'VE GOT AN IDEA!
IF THORN DID SURVIVE, SHE'S NOT GONNA SHAKE US THAT EASY...

YOU CAN DO IT, THORN - -
GET ON YOUR FEET.
THAT'S IT - - - -
NOW **WALK.**
JUST TO THE OTHER **SIDE** . . .
UH, OH. MY HEAD'S GETTING DIZZY.
YOU DO NOT HAVE FAR TO GO.
WHO SAID THAT?
MY NAME WAS TEAR RAHJAN, A FARMER'S DAUGHTER . . .
MY FAMILY AND I WERE REFUGEES TRAPPED INSIDE THE VILLAGE WHEN THE GHOST CIRCLES APPEARED . . .
TEAR RAHJAN - -

I AM TRYING TO REACH TANEN GARD AND FIND THE CROWN OF HORNS.
ONCE I TOUCH THAT SACRED OBJECT, THE GHOST CIRCLES WILL BE UNDONE - - FREEING YOU AND HEALING OUR LAND.
IS THIS TRUE?
YOU CAN BRING US BACK TO LIFE?
IF I CAN, I WILL. BUT I MUST GET THROUGH THE VILLAGE FIRST - -
SSZZKRAK!
WHAT'S THAT?
IT IS THE LOCUST! HE KNOWS YOU ARE HERE!
HELP US.
PAIN.
YOU MUST FLEE!

FOOM!
THE SKY IS ON FIRE!
WE ARE ALL AT HIS MERCY IN THIS PLACE!
YOU HAVE TO LEAVE OR WE WILL BE TURNED TO ASHES!
YOU MUST FLEE!
FLEE!

COMPANY C.! REPORT! DO YOU HAVE ANY PRISONERS?
WE SAW A LONE FEMALE, BUT SHE WAS KILLED WHEN SHE STEPPED INTO A CIRCLE.
NEW MARCHING ORDERS - - YOU'RE GOING TO SINNER'S ROCK TO REINFORCE THE ATTACK ON THE SOUTHERN GATE.
WHEW! WE MADE IT. WE'RE IN THE ENEMY CAMP.
AND WE'RE THROUGH THE GAP!
GOOD JOB, BARTLEBY! NOW HEAD FOR THE MOUNTAINS . . .

HEY! WATCH WHERE YOU'RE GOING -- THERE'RE GHOST CIRCLES AROUND HERE SOMEWHERE!
HOW AM I SUPPOSED TO KNOW WHERE THEY ARE? THEY'RE INVISIBLE!
ffz
ZZTKK!
POW!
FONE BONE! HOW DID YOU AND BARTLEBY GET OUT OF THE CITY?
IT'S A LONG STORY --
SAVE IT. WE DON'T HAVE MUCH TIME.

DO YOU SEE THAT STORM? INSIDE IS THE LOCUST IN THE FORM OF MIM, THE GREAT QUEEN OF THE DRAGONS, AND SHE'S COMING THIS WAY!
WE HAVE TO REACH TANEN GARD AND FIND THE CROWN OF HORNS BEFORE THAT STORM GETS HERE!
BUT IT TOOK US TWO DAYS TO WALK HERE FROM TANEN GARD--
WE'LL TAKE A SHORT-CUT.

BAM!
QUEEN ROSE! THANK THE STARS YOU'VE COME!
THE ENEMY IS USING A BATTERING RAM, AND THE GATE WON'T HOLD MUCH LONGER!
GET EVERYONE BEHIND ME AND GET READY TO OPEN THE GATE ON MY COMMAND!
YOUR MAJESTY - -? ARE YOU SURE WE CAN FIGHT THEM WITH THIS GROUP OF FARMERS?
ARE YOU KIDDING? SHE CAN FIGHT 'EM SINGLE-HANDED IF SHE WANTS!

THEY CERTAINLY WON'T BE EXPECTING IT. AT LEAST SURPRISE IS ON OUR SIDE.
SPEAKING OF SURPRISES, WHAT ARE YOU DOING HERE, PHONEY BONE?
NEXT TO YOU? SAFEST PLACE IN THE WHOLE WAR.
BAM!
THAT GATE'S ABOUT TO GO! FALL IN!
YOU MEN BEHIND ME -- GO STRAIGHT FOR THE ARMED SOLDIERS WAITING TO RUSH IN!
THIS ISN'T A GAME, SO KILL YOUR ENEMY!
BAM
MERMIE, YOU HANDLE THE BOYS ON THE BATTERING RAM.
OF COURSE.
GULP.
MAYBE THIS ISN'T SUCH A --
NOW!
AAAH!

LOOK OUT! TWO GOT THROUGH!
AR! SNAR!
STOP THEM! DON'T LET THEM IN THE CITY!
RRAAH! SSS!
RARRAR!
PLEASE DON'T HURT US! IT'S NOT OUR FAULT WE'RE MONSTERS! WE WERE BORN THIS WAY!
HEY! I KNOW THESE GUYS!

AAAIE
CANG!
SHING!
YEAH! YEAH!
WE'RE ROUTIN' `EM!
MERMIE! LADDERS!
LOOK AT `EM RUN!
RUN BACK TO YOUR MISTRESS! TELL HER TO COME **HERSELF** NEXT TIME!

Huff! Puff!
BREAK THOSE LADDERS INTO PIECES AND GET THIS GATE RE-BARRED...

Puff! Puff.

Huff...

EYUH!

WOULD YOU LIKE TO GO HOME NOW, PHONCIBLE P. BONE?
WHAT?
NOT FAR FROM WHERE WE ARE STANDING IS THE ENTRANCE TO A SECRET TUNNEL THAT WILL TAKE YOU PAST THE GHOST CIRCLES AND UP TO THE MOUNTAINS . . . YOU CAN LEAVE FOR BONEVILLE.
THE TUNNEL IS REAL. IF YOU WANT TO GO, ANSWER QUICKLY.
I - - DON'T - -
I CAN'T LEAVE WITHOUT MY COUSINS.
GOOD. JUST CHECKING.
COME WITH ME.
JUST CHECKING?!

YOU WERE **TESTING** ME?
YES.
THERE.
THIS ESCAPE TUNNEL ONCE BELONGED TO THE ROYAL FAMILY. THE ORIGINAL ENTRANCE WAS DESTROYED LONG AGO.
WHERE ARE WE GOING?
TO SEE MY **SISTER**.

I HATE SHORTCUTS.
STOP WORRYING. THIS TRENCH **HAS** TO FEED INTO THE BURIAL GROUND GORGE **SOMEWHERE.**
hmmf.
WAIT - - !
YOUR **FRIEND** IS CURLED UP IN THE MIDDLE OF THE PATH.
WHO?
TAKE A LOOK.

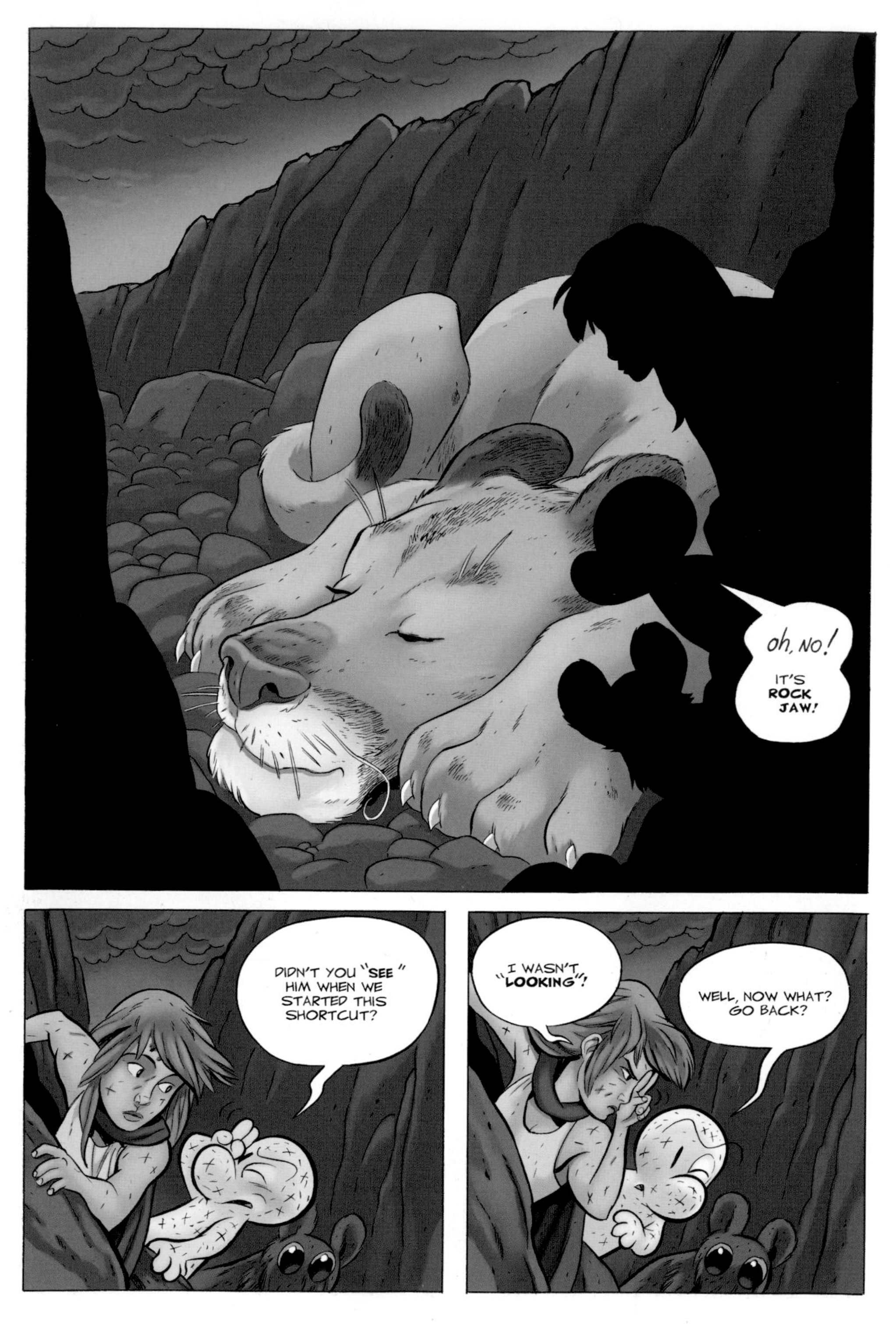
oh, NO! IT'S ROCK JAW!
DIDN'T YOU "SEE" HIM WHEN WE STARTED THIS SHORTCUT?
I WASN'T "LOOKING"!
WELL, NOW WHAT? GO BACK?

NO, WE DON'T HAVE TIME. WE'LL HAVE TO SNEAK PAST HIM.
SNEAK PAST A CAT?
WE'LL GO ONE AT A TIME. AND BE CAREFUL NOT TO TOUCH HIS WHISKERS!
YOU GONNA BE OKAY, BARTLEBY?
I'M NOT AFRAID! I'M NOT SCARED OF ANYTHING - -
EXCEPT DRAGONS.
RIGHT. LET'S GO.

RUN, FONE BONE!
WAIT!
PUT YOUR SWORD AWAY.
BARTLEBY... COME OVER TO US...
SLOWLY...

C'MON, HE'S LETTIN' US GO.
HUFF! PUFF!
HOLD UP.
WE MADE IT.
I THINK - HUFF - THIS IS THE PLATEAU . . .
LOOK, THORN!

YES! JUST BEYOND THOSE PEAKS IS THE BOTTOMLESS PIT OF TANEN GARD - - THE DRAGONS' SACRED BURIAL GROUND.
BUT LOOK AT THE **ARMY** THAT'S WAITING TO STOP US!
BRIAR KNEW WE WOULD COME HERE TO FIND THE CROWN OF HORNS.
WHAT DO WE DO? ROCK JAW IS BEHIND US!
TO GET PAST THE ARMY, I'LL NEED A DISTRACTION - -
WHOA - - !
LET'S TALK ABOUT THIS A SECOND!
I'M GOING IN, FONE BONE.
YOU CAN HELP ME OR NOT.
I'LL HELP.

OKAY, THEN. YOU AND BARTLEBY WORK YOUR WAY ALONG THESE ROCKS . . . .
. . . TRY TO GET AS CLOSE TO THE ARMY AS YOU CAN, THEN MAKE SOME NOISE! LEAD AS MANY AS POSSIBLE INTO THE MOUNTAINS.
WHILE THEY'RE LOOKING AT YOU, I'LL SLIP INTO THEIR CAMP.
GO - - BEFORE YOU HAVE TIME TO THINK!
C'MON, BONE!
ooh.
I HATE THIS PLAN.
IT'S A TERRIBLE PLAN . . .

. . . SHE'S GOING INTO THE DRAGON'S GRAVEYARD **ALONE!**
AND **WE'LL** BE STUCK RUNNING AROUND THE MOUNTAINS WITH AN **ARMY** ON OUR BUTTS!
STAY BEHIND THE ROCKS!
WHAT AM I **DOING?!** I CAN'T LET HER GO ALONE - -
YOU KNOW WHAT? I'M GOIN' **BACK.** THIS IS A **TERRIBLE** PLAN - -
FONE BONE! LOOK!
THORN'S WALKING OUT TO MEET THEM HEAD-ON!
WHAT?

SHE CAN'T! THEY'LL SEE HER!

TOO LATE!

STOP!

IT'S JUST LIKE A DREAM . . .
LOOK! A BONE CREATURE!

DID YOU SEE THAT?!
BONE! THEY'RE COMING!
SHE FLEW INTO THE DRAGONS' GRAVEYARD WITHOUT ME!!
PLEASE! WE HAVE TO GET OUT OF HERE!
SHE CAN'T DO THAT TO ME!! COME ON! WE'RE GOING IN AFTER HER!!
OKAY! JUST HURRY!
AAAA!
A PIECE OF GOLD TO THE ONE WHO KILLS THE BONE CREATURE!

WE MADE IT!
THORN!
DO YOU SMELL THAT? IT'S **BRIMSTONE.**
THORN!
THERE ARE DRAGONS **EVERYWHERE!**
WE HAVE TO GO IN - -
IT'S TOO DANGEROUS! THE DRAGONS WILL **KILL US!**
YOU STAY HERE.
I'LL GO.
NO, NO. I'M COMING.
IT'S OKAY. WAIT HERE FOR ME . . .

I'M JUST GONNA GET THORN AND BE RIGHT BACK.
I'M SORRY, BONE . . .
BE CAREFUL - - THE DRAGONS ARE REALLY ANGRY!

BONE®
♪
SMILEY BONE!
WHAT ARE YOU DOING?
I THOUGHT YOU WERE WATCHING THE PRISONERS!
I'M DOING BETTER THAN THAT- - I'M BAKING THEM A QUICHE!
YOU'RE BAKING FOR THEM WHILE WE'RE UNDER SIEGE?! BUT WE HAVE A FOOD SHORTAGE!
I KNOW!

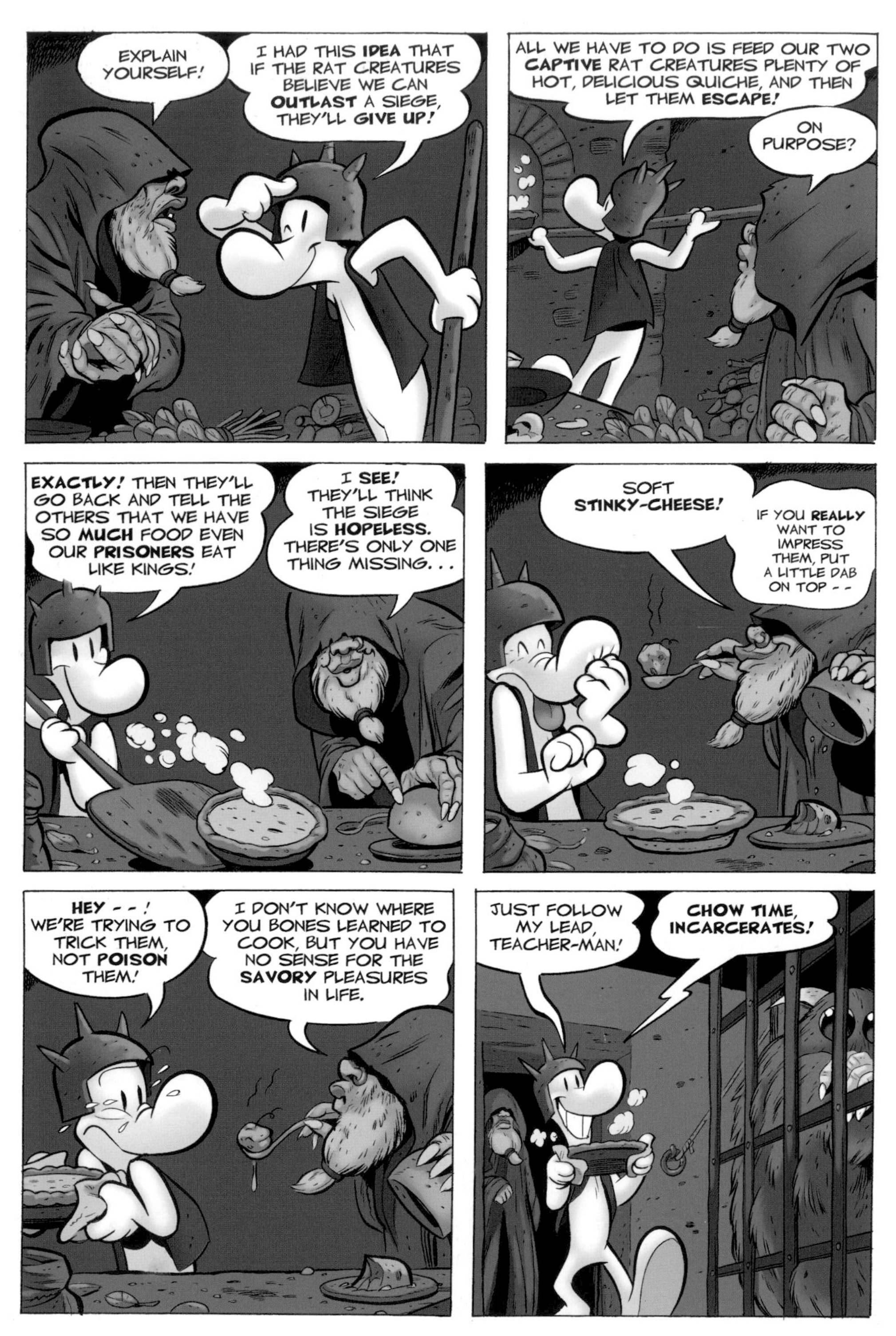
EXPLAIN YOURSELF!
I HAD THIS IDEA THAT IF THE RAT CREATURES BELIEVE WE CAN OUTLAST A SIEGE, THEY'LL GIVE UP!
ALL WE HAVE TO DO IS FEED OUR TWO CAPTIVE RAT CREATURES PLENTY OF HOT, DELICIOUS QUICHE, AND THEN LET THEM ESCAPE!
ON PURPOSE?
EXACTLY! THEN THEY'LL GO BACK AND TELL THE OTHERS THAT WE HAVE SO MUCH FOOD EVEN OUR PRISONERS EAT LIKE KINGS!
I SEE! THEY'LL THINK THE SIEGE IS HOPELESS. THERE'S ONLY ONE THING MISSING. . .
SOFT STINKY-CHEESE!
IF YOU REALLY WANT TO IMPRESS THEM, PUT A LITTLE DAB ON TOP - -
HEY - - ! WE'RE TRYING TO TRICK THEM, NOT POISON THEM!
I DON'T KNOW WHERE YOU BONES LEARNED TO COOK, BUT YOU HAVE NO SENSE FOR THE SAVORY PLEASURES IN LIFE.
JUST FOLLOW MY LEAD, TEACHER-MAN!
CHOW TIME, INCARCERATES!

HERE YOU GO, FELLAS. PIPING HOT... RIGHT OUT OF THE OVEN!
IS --
IS THAT WHAT I THINK IT IS?
IT'S YOUR FAVORITE! CUSTARD PIE WITH CHEESE AND BACON!
QUICHE!
NO, COMRADE!! BE STRONG!
MONSTERS DON'T EAT FLAKEY BAKERY PRODUCTS! GET A HOLD OF YOURSELF!
BUT COMRADE, I'M STARVING! OUR ARMY HAS NO FOOD! WE HAVEN'T EATEN SINCE THE GHOST CIRCLES APPEARED!
OH, WELL! WE CERTAINLY HAVE A LOT OF FOOD HERE, DON'T WE, TEACH? A LOT OF FOOD...
OH, YES! A LOT OF FOOD!
OKAY! I GIVE UP! YES! YES!! GIVE US THE QUICHE!! WE'RE STARVING--
MASTER! COME RIGHT AWAY!
A GREAT CLOUD FILLS THE SKY, AND SOMETHING LARGE IS MOVING INSIDE IT!
HAVE YOU ALERTED QUEEN ROSE?

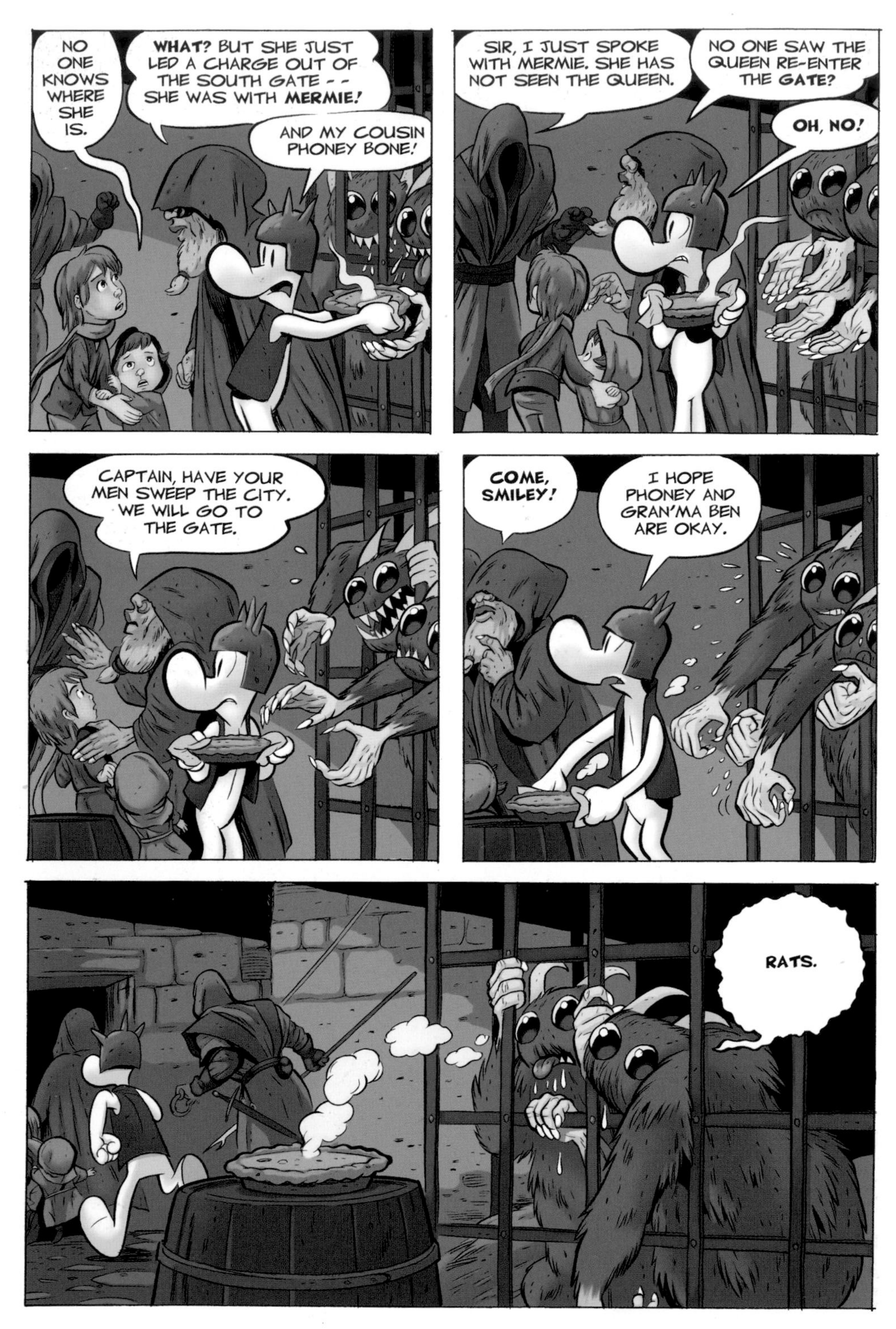
NO ONE KNOWS WHERE SHE IS.
WHAT? BUT SHE JUST LED A CHARGE OUT OF THE SOUTH GATE - - SHE WAS WITH MERMIE!
AND MY COUSIN PHONEY BONE!
SIR, I JUST SPOKE WITH MERMIE. SHE HAS NOT SEEN THE QUEEN.
NO ONE SAW THE QUEEN RE-ENTER THE GATE?
OH, NO!
CAPTAIN, HAVE YOUR MEN SWEEP THE CITY. WE WILL GO TO THE GATE.
COME, SMILEY!
I HOPE PHONEY AND GRAN'MA BEN ARE OKAY.
RATS.

ARE YOU SURE THIS IS A GOOD IDEA, GRAN'MA?
PATIENCE, PHONCIBLE . . .
WE'RE NEAR THE DIVERGENCE NOW.
THERE IT IS! THE TWO TUNNELS . . .
THE ROAD TO THE LEFT GOES TO THE MOUNTAINS, AND EVENTUALLY BACK TO THE PASS THAT BROUGHT YOU HERE FROM BONEVILLE.
IT ALSO LEADS TO DEREN GARD.
IT'S THE PATH THORN AND HER PARENTS TOOK THE NIGHT THEY WERE AMBUSHED.
WHERE DOES THE ROAD TO THE RIGHT GO?
TO SINNER'S ROCK . . .
AND MY SISTER.
LET'S GO.
ARE WE GONNA FIGHT YOUR SISTER AND THE RAT CREATURES BY OURSELVES?
NOT IF TED DELIVERED MY MESSAGE.
WITH ANY LUCK, LUCIUS AND THE VENI-YAN WARRIORS WILL MEET US THERE . . .

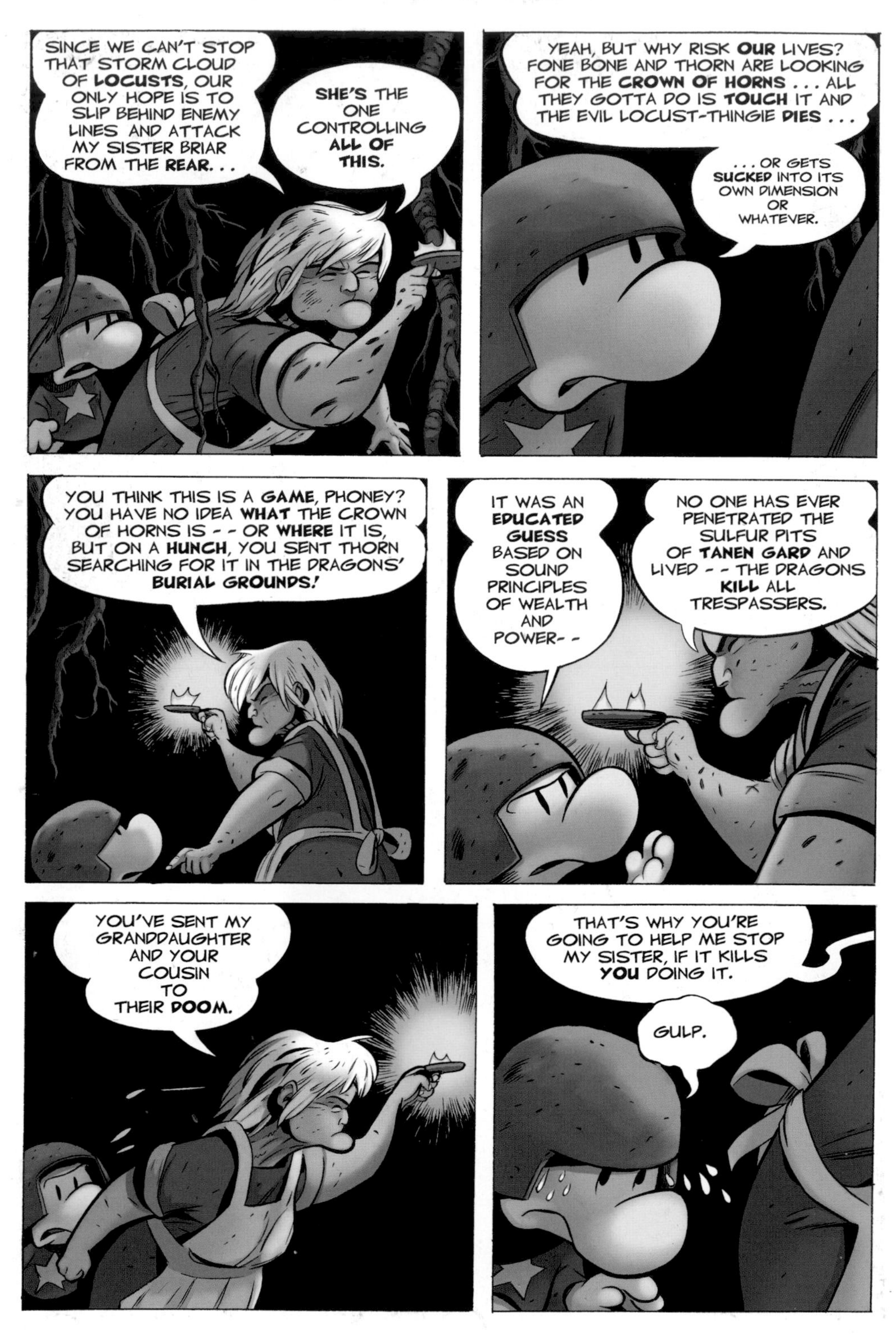
SINCE WE CAN'T STOP THAT STORM CLOUD OF LOCUSTS, OUR ONLY HOPE IS TO SLIP BEHIND ENEMY LINES AND ATTACK MY SISTER BRIAR FROM THE REAR. . .
SHE'S THE ONE CONTROLLING ALL OF THIS.
YEAH, BUT WHY RISK OUR LIVES? FONE BONE AND THORN ARE LOOKING FOR THE CROWN OF HORNS . . . ALL THEY GOTTA DO IS TOUCH IT AND THE EVIL LOCUST-THINGIE DIES . . .
. . . OR GETS SUCKED INTO ITS OWN DIMENSION OR WHATEVER.
YOU THINK THIS IS A GAME, PHONEY? YOU HAVE NO IDEA WHAT THE CROWN OF HORNS IS - - OR WHERE IT IS, BUT ON A HUNCH, YOU SENT THORN SEARCHING FOR IT IN THE DRAGONS' BURIAL GROUNDS!
IT WAS AN EDUCATED GUESS BASED ON SOUND PRINCIPLES OF WEALTH AND POWER- -
NO ONE HAS EVER PENETRATED THE SULFUR PITS OF TANEN GARD AND LIVED - - THE DRAGONS KILL ALL TRESPASSERS.
YOU'VE SENT MY GRANDDAUGHTER AND YOUR COUSIN TO THEIR DOOM.
THAT'S WHY YOU'RE GOING TO HELP ME STOP MY SISTER, IF IT KILLS YOU DOING IT.
GULP.

THORN?
SHUH SHUH
SHUHSH
SHUHSH
GURGLE

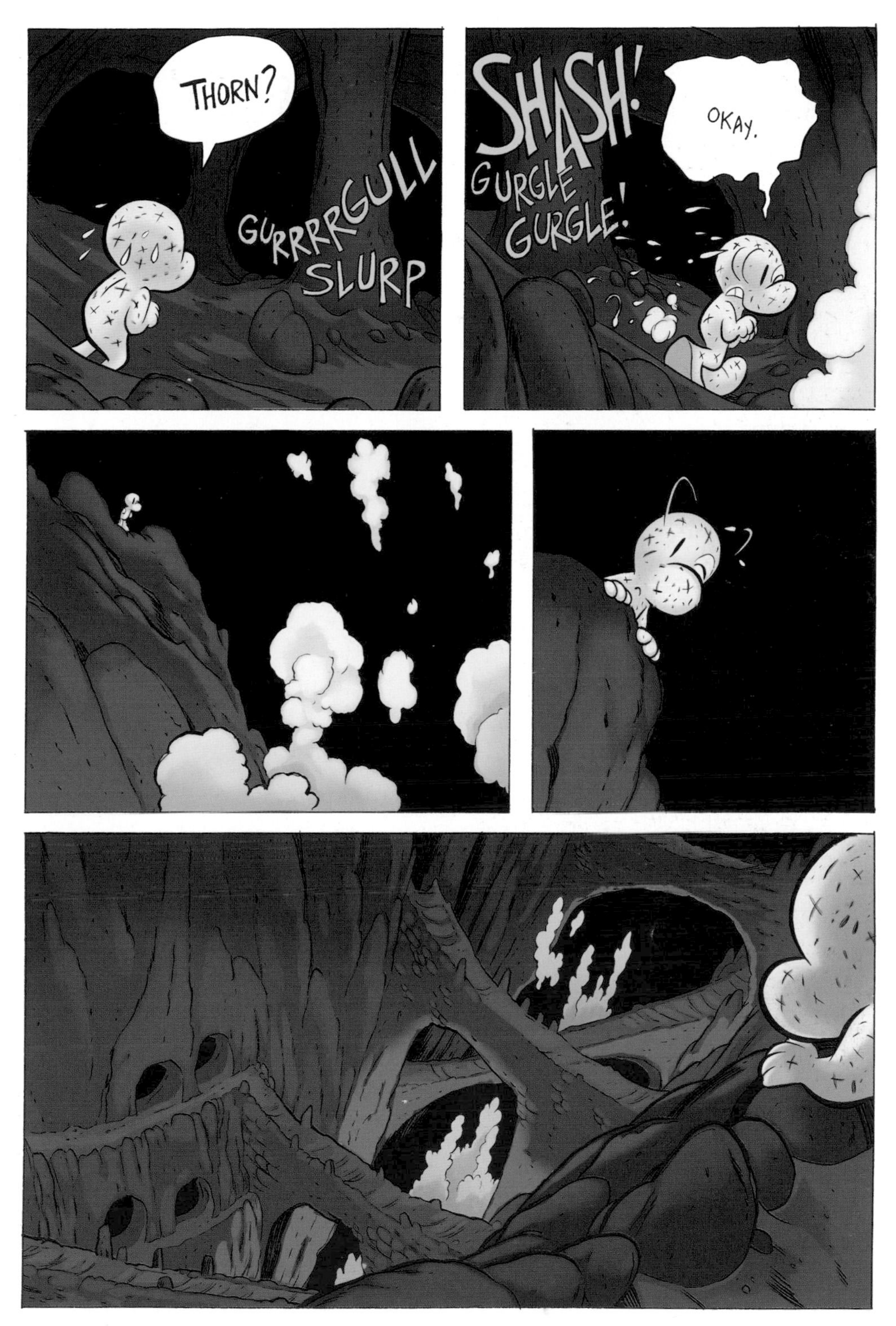
THORN?
GURRRRGULL
SLURP
SHASH!
GURGLE
GURGLE!
OKAY.

!
THERE SHE IS!
HEY, THORN --
SHUH
GURGLE!
SPLASH!
ROAR!

RAHSH
DAA!
I CAN'T GET OUT.
HEY! THORN--

WAIT! WHAT'S THAT?
BARTLEBY?!
WHOA! AM I GLAD TO SEE YOU - -

UH, OH.

ALL RIGHT, THIS IS THE EXIT TO SINNER'S ROCK, SO BE CAREFUL.
WE'RE BEHIND ENEMY LINES NOW --
OOPS.
AH, ROSE ..... MY SISTER ...
YOU MUST WONDER HOW I DO IT... HOW I OUTSMART YOU AGAIN AND AGAIN ....
WOULD YOU LIKE TO KNOW MY SECRET?

EVER SINCE I WAS A LITTLE GIRL I COULD HEAR THE LOCUST WHISPERING TO ME INSIDE MY HEAD . . . . DO YOU KNOW WHAT THAT'S LIKE . . . ?
IT'S LIKE BEING THE SMARTEST PERSON IN ALL THE WORLD . . . . . .
MMMMMMM.
AND **YES**, I KNOW WHAT YOUR PRECIOUS GRANDDAUGHTER IS UP TO . . . . BUT SHE WILL NEVER REACH THE CROWN OF HORNS ALIVE . . . .
AS I ANTICIPATED **YOUR** EVERY MOVE . . .
SO HAVE I ANTICIPATED **HERS** . . .
MMMM.

SSSHHHHHH

SHHHHH
SHUH SHUH

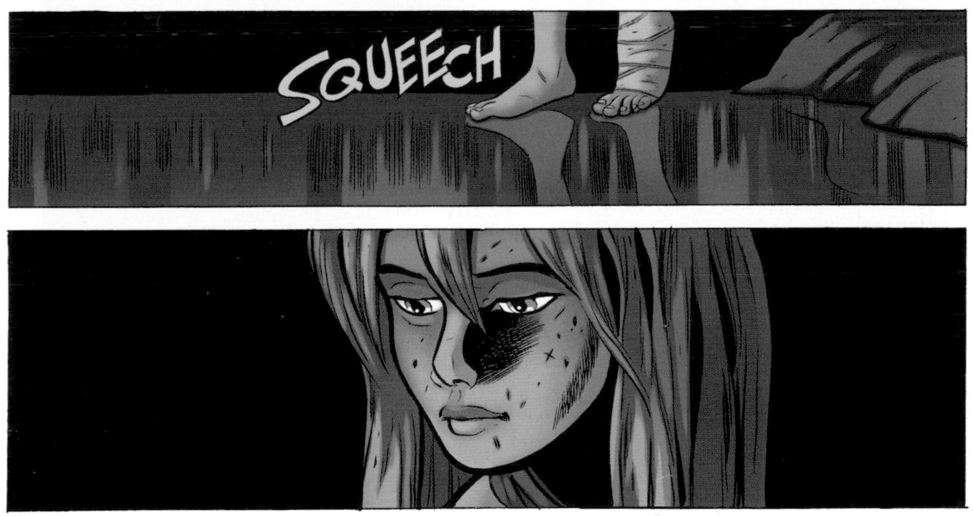
SQUEECH

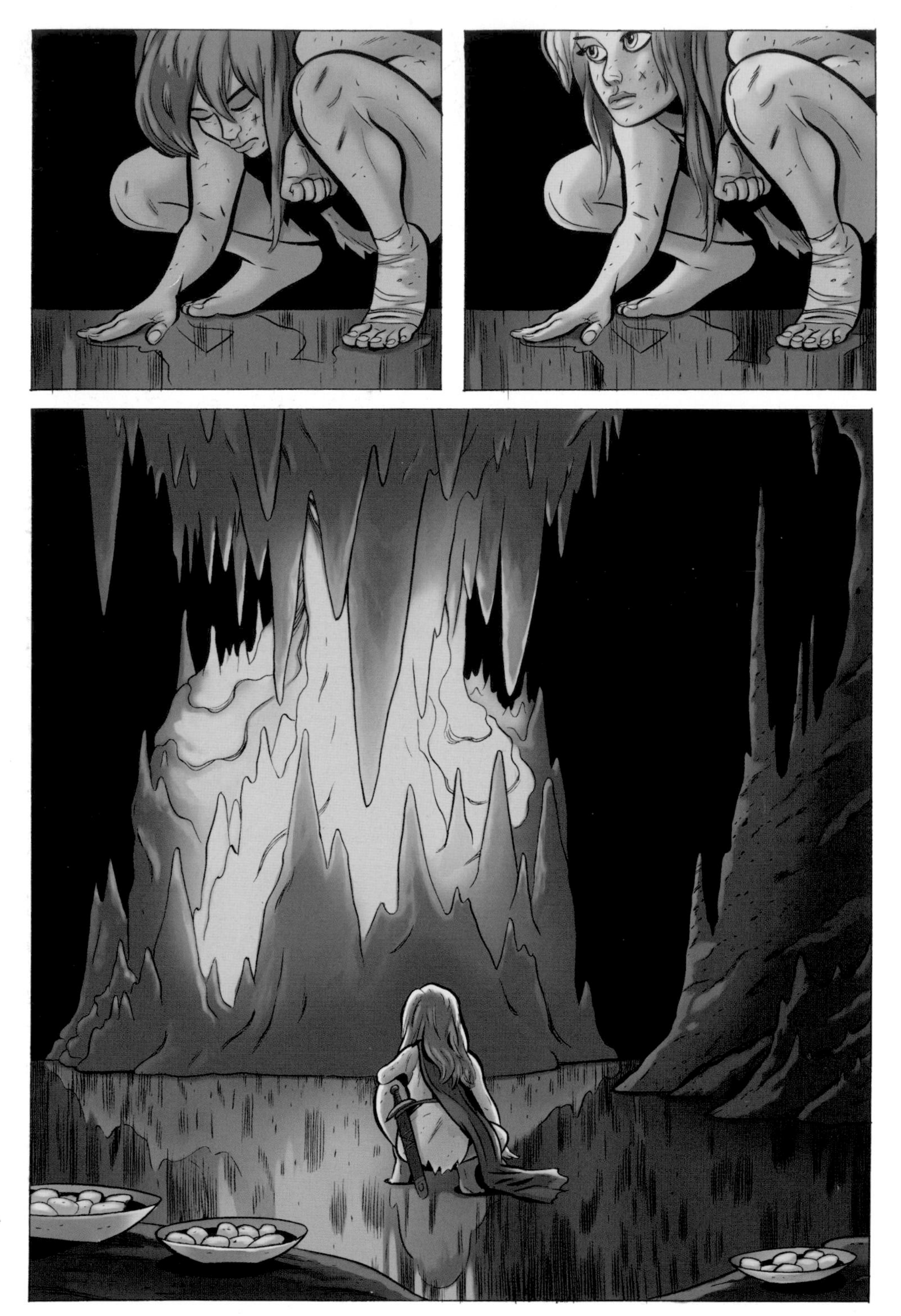

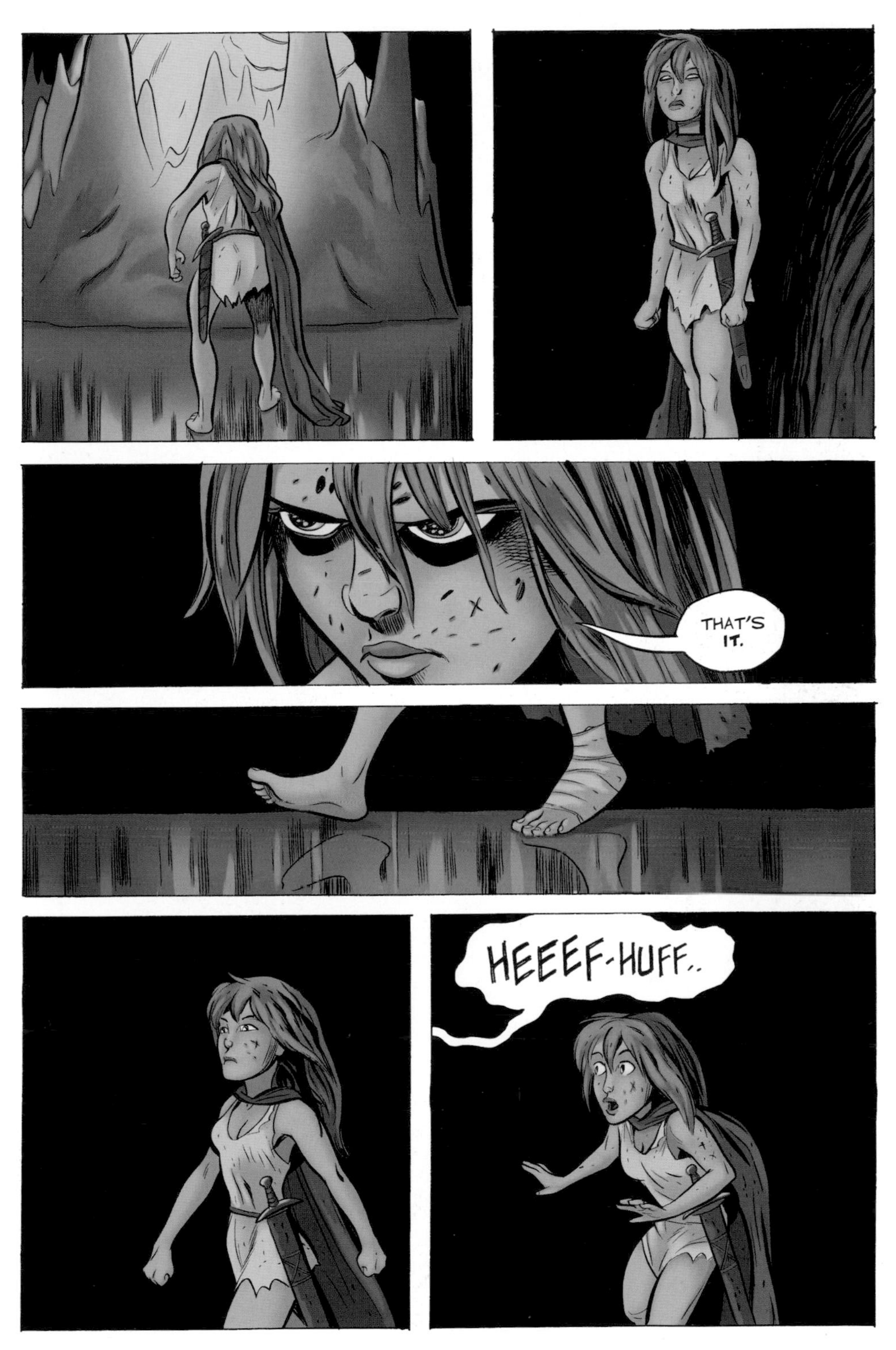
THAT'S IT.
HEEEF-HUFF..

SSSSSSS
RRRRRRRRRR
Hfff... wheez
Huff.. wheez
Huff..
Wheeez..
TO TOUCH THE CROWN OF HORNS . . . YOU WILL HAVE TO GO THROUGH ME.

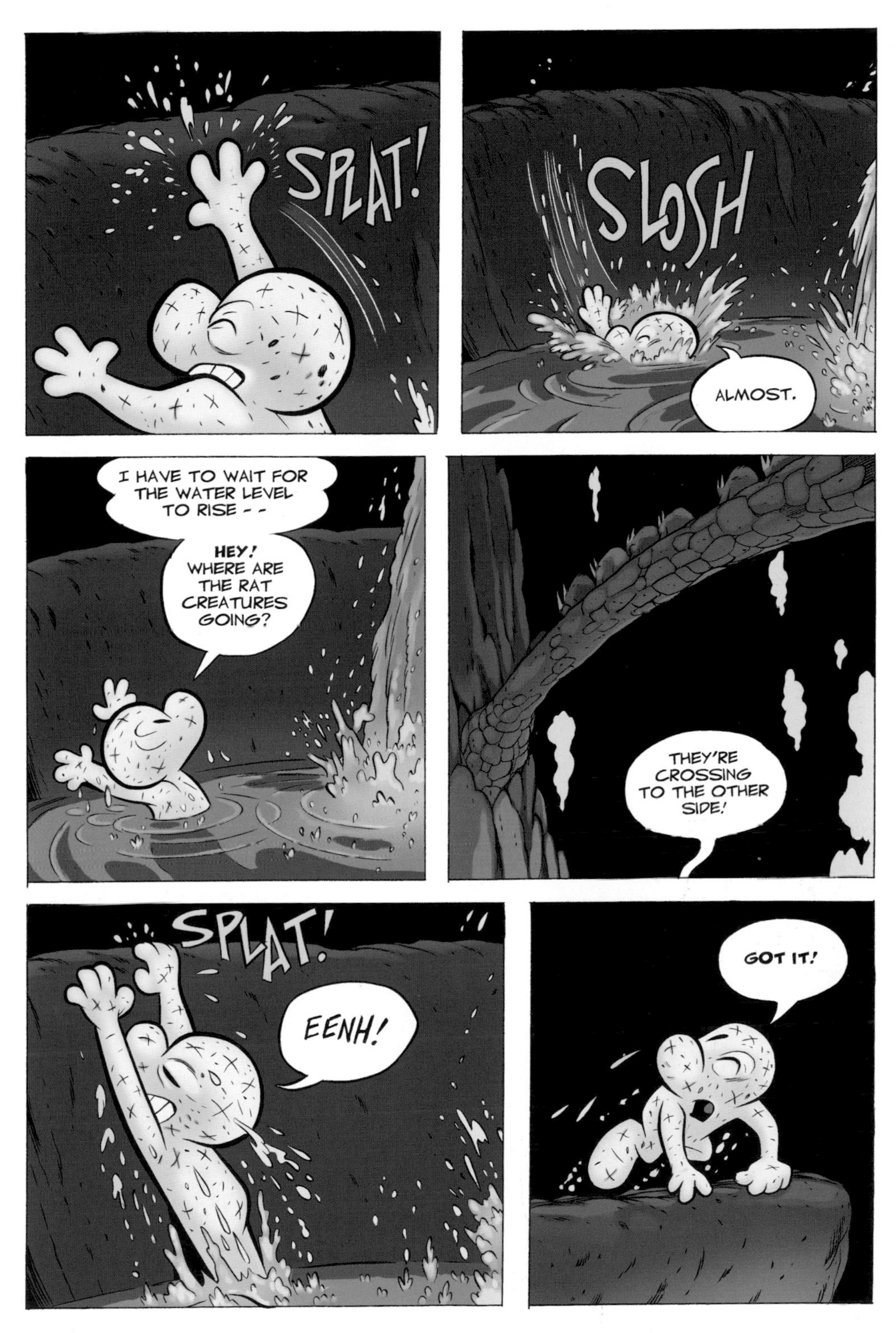
SPLAT!
SLOSH
ALMOST.
I HAVE TO WAIT FOR THE WATER LEVEL TO RISE - -
HEY! WHERE ARE THE RAT CREATURES GOING?
THEY'RE CROSSING TO THE OTHER SIDE!
SPLAT!
EENH!
GOT IT!

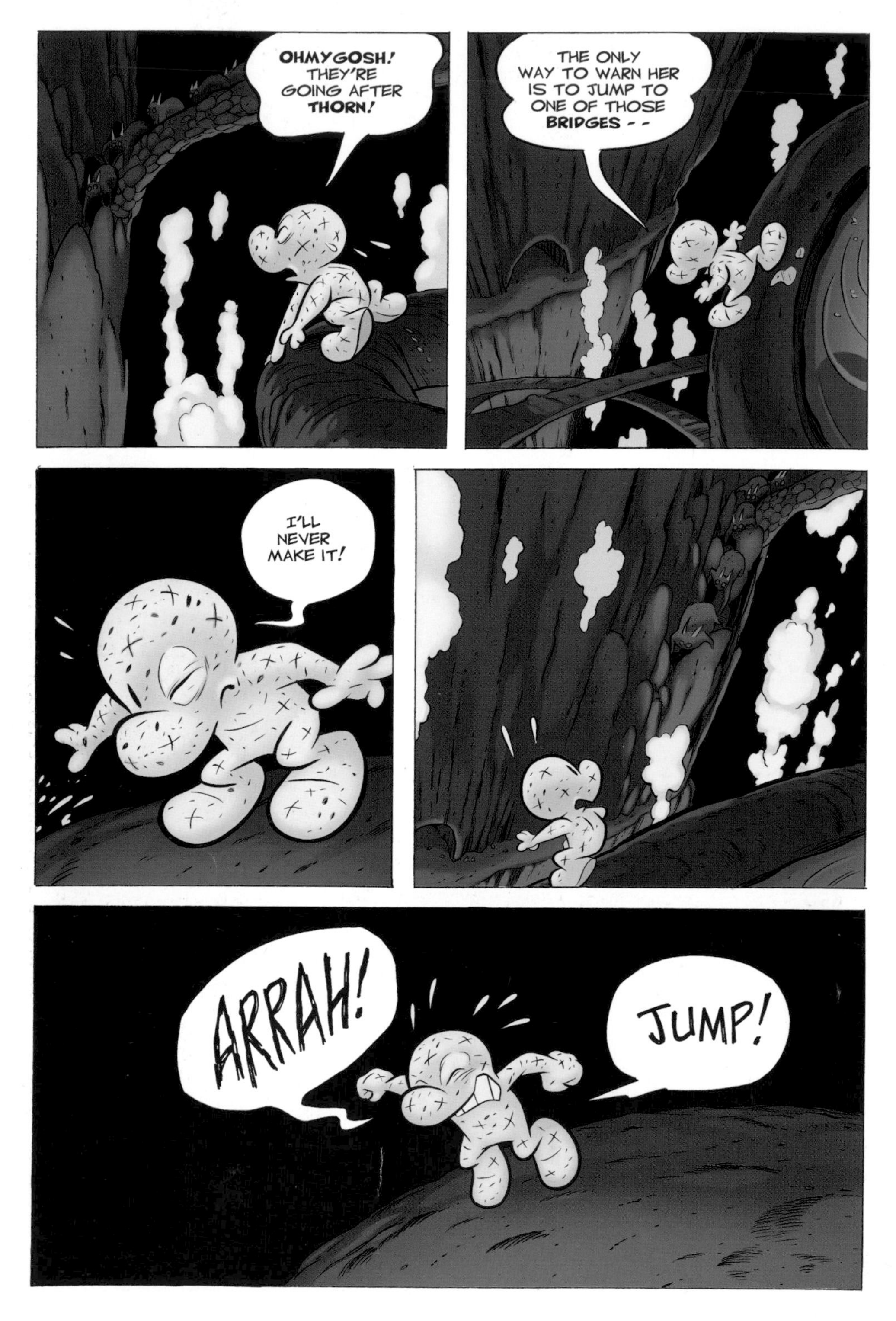
OHMYGOSH! THEY'RE GOING AFTER THORN!
THE ONLY WAY TO WARN HER IS TO JUMP TO ONE OF THOSE BRIDGES --
I'LL NEVER MAKE IT!
ARRAH!
JUMP!

HEEEF
HUFF
LET ME PASS, KINGDOK.
YOU MUST KILL ME IN ORDER TO REACH THE CROWN.
IT IS THE ONLY WAY.
WHY DO YOU STOP ME?
THE VALLEY IS BEING DESTROYED. THE LOCUST HAS BETRAYED BOTH OUR PEOPLE.
LOOK AT ME... I WAS ONCE A MIGHTY KING-- NOW I AM A SLAVE--A PUPPET WITH NO WILL OF MY OWN...
EITHER YOU KILL ME OR I KILL YOU!

SHUNK!
I WILL NOT KILL YOU.
NOW FOR THE GOOD OF OUR PEOPLE, STAND ASIDE.
KILL ME!
NO.
I WAS THE ONE WHO ATE YOUR PARENTS. I FED ON YOUR MOTHER WHILE SHE WAS STILL ALIVE.

HEEEF... HUFF...
HEEEF...
I HAVE TO TOUCH THE CROWN OF HORNS.
AAH!

AAA
SHIIING!

CRRASH!

ERR-
EEUN-

HA HA HA HA HA HA
HA
HA HA HA HA HA HA HA
THE LOCUST IS HERE.
GOOD-BYE, ROSE.

MOTHER ALWAYS DID LIKE YOU BEST.
CRIINGG!
CRASH!
HOLD STILL!

KRAK!
BAH BOOM!

SSSSSSSSSSHHH
THORN?
WHERE ARE YOU?
HERE I AM!
WHAT HAPPENED?
KINGDOK IS DEAD. GET HIM OFF ME!
HIS JAWS WON'T BUDGE - -
AAH.
WE HAVE TO GET YOU OUT - - RAT CREATURES ARE COMING RIGHT BEHIND ME!

HELP ME TOUCH THE CROWN OF HORNS FIRST.
WHERE IS IT?
THIS! I HAVE TO REACH IT...
THE WALL?
THE WALL IS THE CROWN OF HORNS? THAT'S NOT WHAT I PICTURED.
I'LL DO IT.
WHAT?
I'LL TOUCH IT. I HAVE THE LOCUST INSIDE ME, TOO.

NOTHING HAPPENED.
WAS SOMETHING SUPPOSED TO HAPPEN?
NOTHING HAPPENED!!
I TOOK THE LOCUST OUT OF YOU . . .
WHAT?!
WHEN WE WERE INSIDE THE GHOST CIRCLE TOGETHER, I TOOK THE PIECE OF LOCUST AWAY FROM YOU.
WELL, GIVE IT BACK - -
SKITTER SKITTER

SPANG!
POW!
HAA!
YAA!
THP!
THWIIIP!
THUMP!
INTRUDERS!!
SHIING!
SHIING!
SHIING!
SHIING

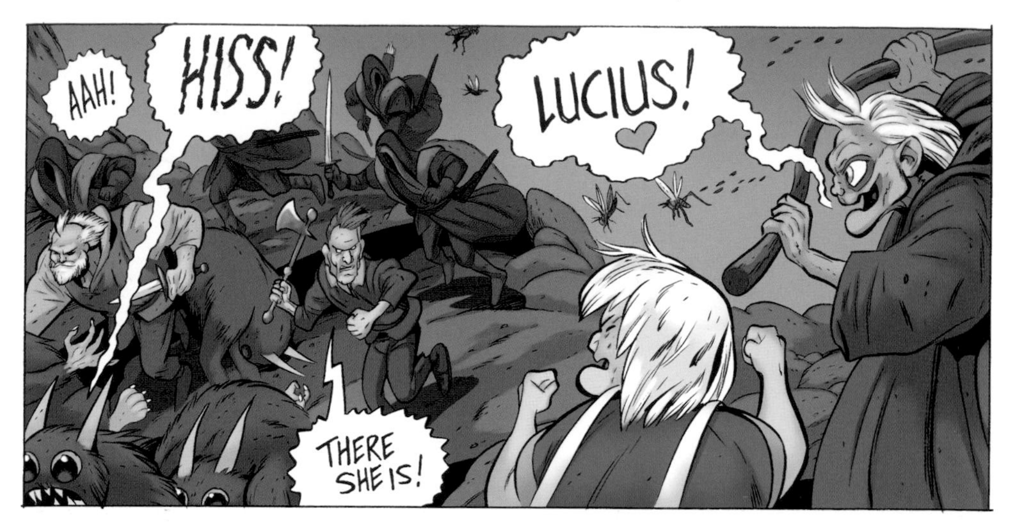
AAH!
HISS!
LUCIUS!
THERE SHE IS!

SHOOT THE WITCH!
THP!
THWANG!

TWEEEEEE

SPING!
KOW!
PINNG!

AAAH!

ROSE!
HA! HA!
UHH..
HA HA HA HA
HA HA HA HA HA HA HA HA HA HA HA
HAAA HA HA HAHA

GIVE IT BACK! HURRY!
I'M TRYING! IT WON'T LEAVE!
STOP THEM!
GIVE IT NOW!!
I CAN'T! WE HAVE TO KILL IT WHILE IT'S STILL INSIDE ME!
OKAY, THEN - - HOLD MY HAND TIGHT!
EENH...
SHUFFLE

SHUFF SHUFF
WHAT ARE YOU DOING?!
BUILDING UP A STATIC CHARGE FOR LUCK.
SNAP!

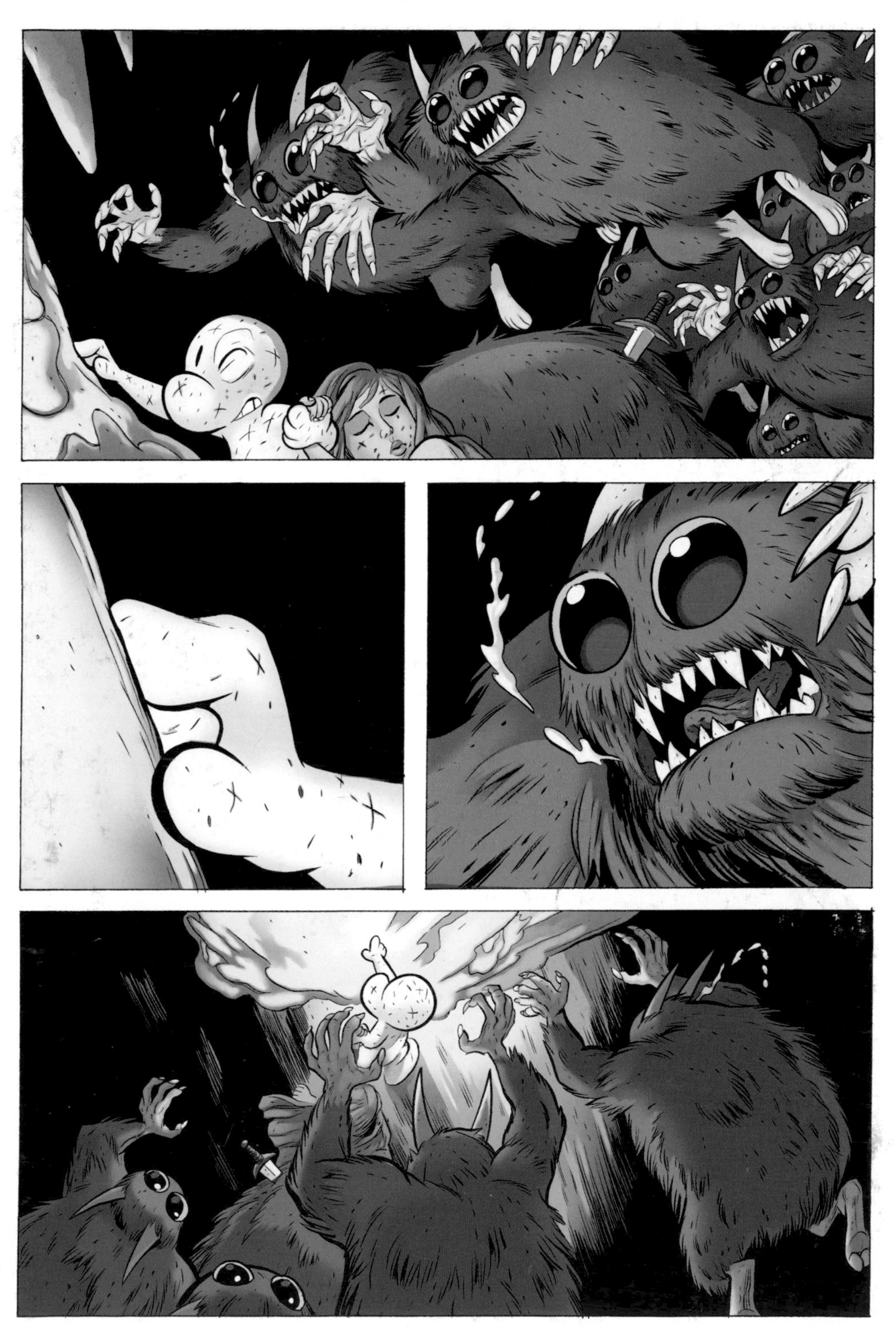

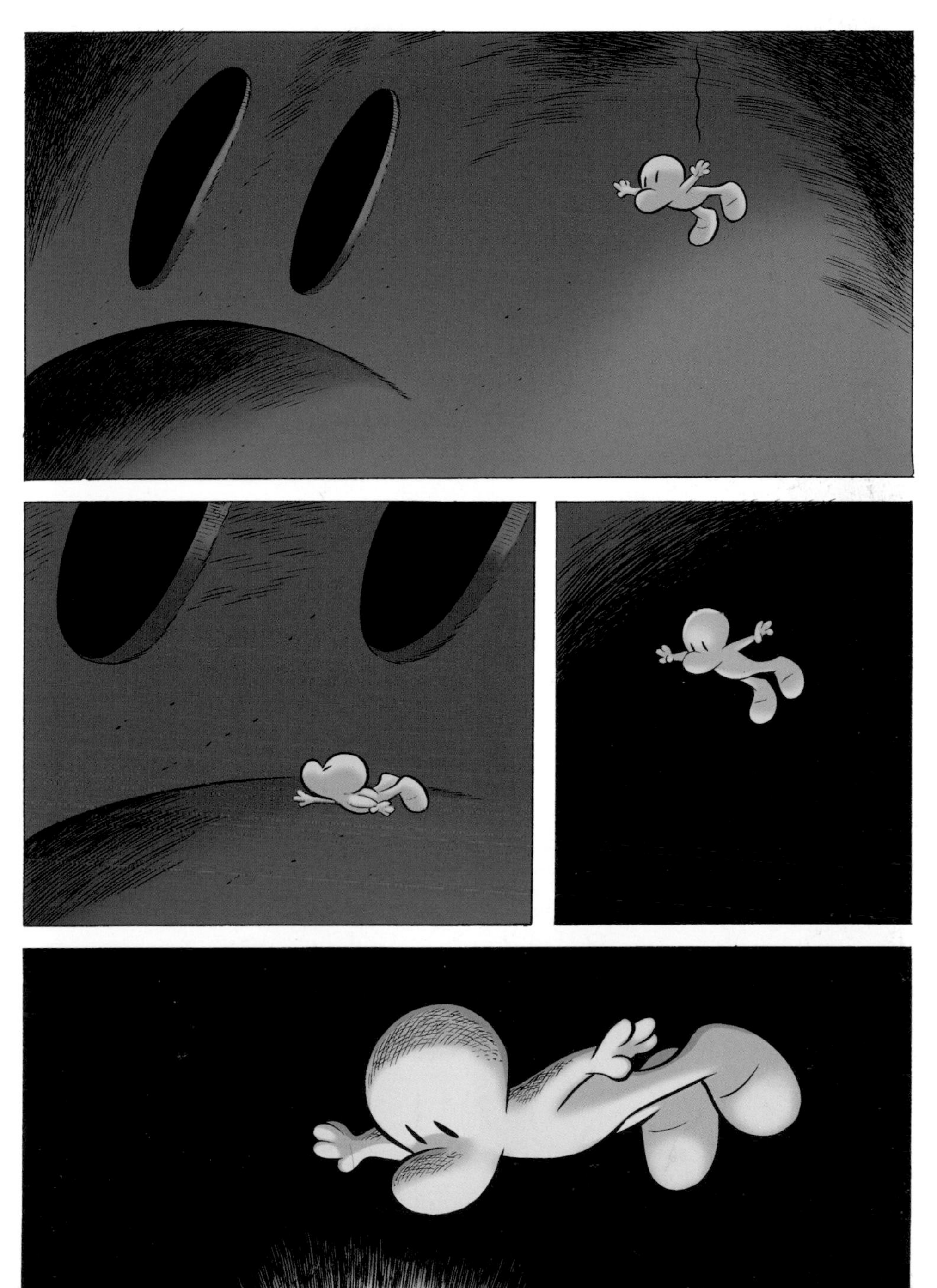

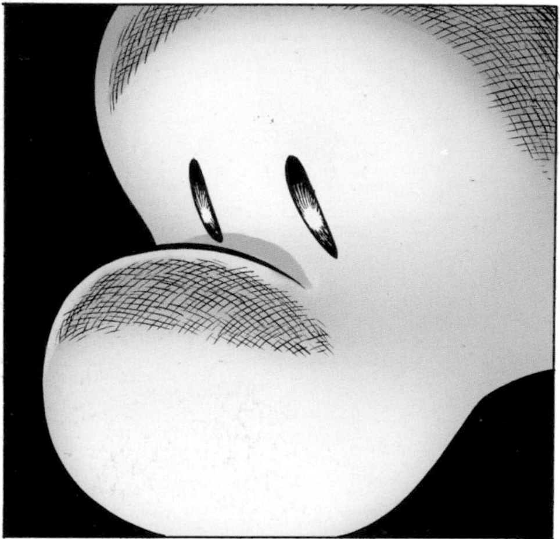

HELLO.

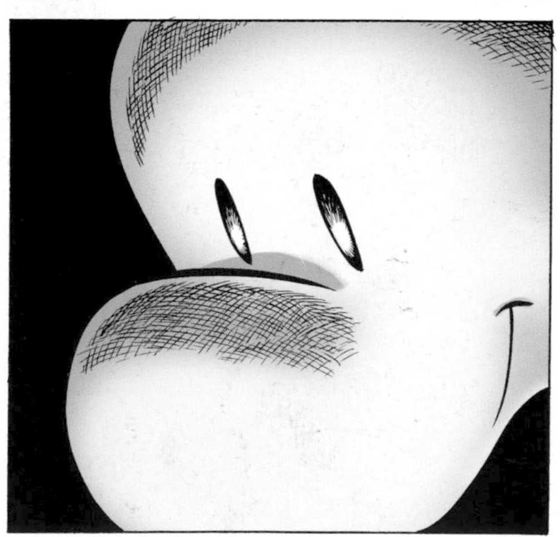

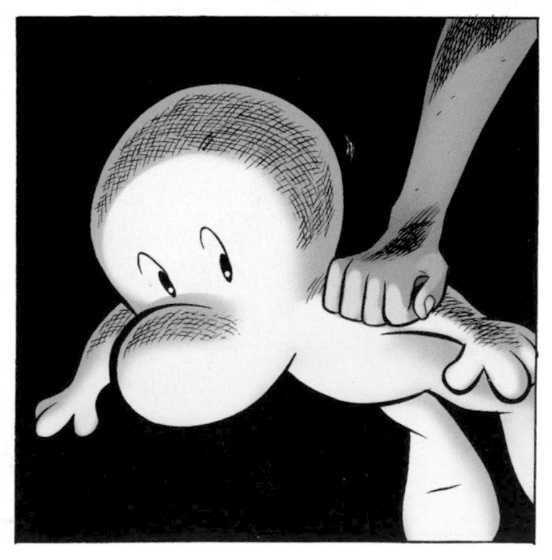

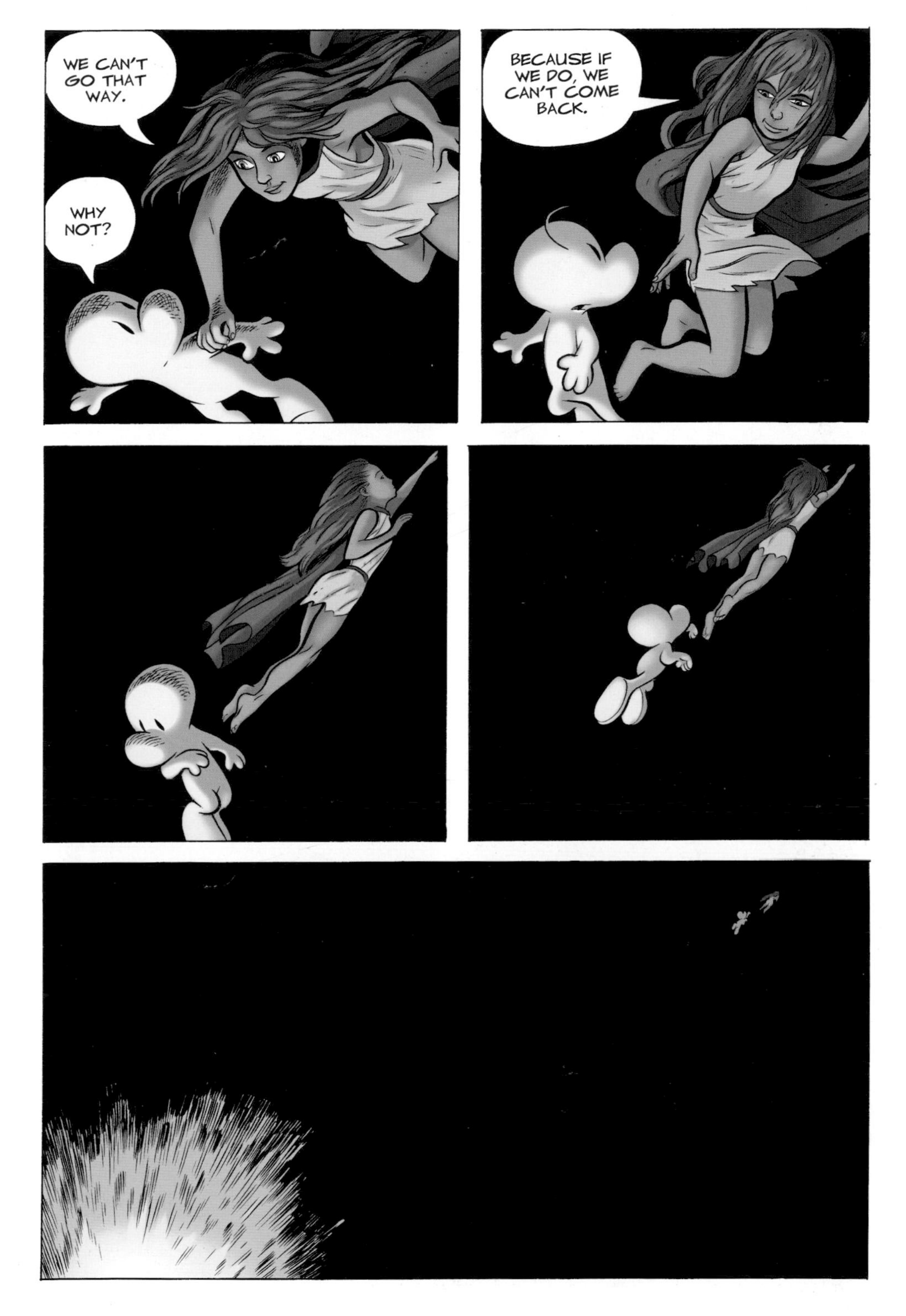
WE CAN'T GO THAT WAY.
WHY NOT?
BECAUSE IF WE DO, WE CAN'T COME BACK.

THE STORM CLOUD IS BREAKING UP!
AND THE RAT CREATURES ARE RETREATING!
THE LOCUST IS DEAD!
VICTORY IS OURS!
HISSSSS!
I HAVE MEDICINE FOR THE QUEEN - -

YOUR MAJESTY, ARE YOU HURT- -?
THEY MADE IT. . .
DID YOU HEAR THAT, LUCIUS? THE CHILDREN FOUND THE CROWN OF HORNS.

FONE BONE--
WAKE UP! WE HAVE TO GO!
RUMMBLE
WHAT HAPPENED? WHERE ARE THE RAT CREATURES?
HOLY SMOKES! WHAT'S GOING ON? IT FEELS LIKE AN EARTHQUAKE --
IT'S THE DRAGONS! THEY'RE COMING FROM ALL DIRECTIONS! THAT'S WHY THE RAT CREATURES LEFT!
COMING HERE?! WHY?
WE WOKE THEM UP AND THEY'RE ANGRY.
HOW MANY DRAGONS DID WE WAKE UP?
ALL OF THEM.
ALL OF THEM. . . OH, BOY.
HURRY, FONE BONE. I'M STARTING TO GET SCARED.

NOW YOU'RE STARTING TO GET SCARED?
TRY USING THE SWORD.
UNH!
SLISH
PLOP
AAAH!
SPLASH
OH, NO. YOUR LEG . . .
RIPP
HANG ON, I'LL WRAP IT REAL TIGHT - -
DON'T.
LEAVE ME, I'VE FINISHED WHAT I CAME FOR.
OH, NO, NO, NO. GET UP!

WE'LL BE OKAY, YOU'LL SEE!
NO . . . THE DRAGONS WILL KILL US . . .
KREE! KREE!
KAAAAA!
COME ON, COME ON . . .
SKREE!
SPLASH!
NO--
NO! THORN, WAKE UP!
RRREEEAH!
TK TK TK TK
PLEASE WAKE UP . . .
RUMMBLLEEE

CRASH
KAA!
RAAAAH!
uunh...
KREEE!
FUM! FUN
KREE KREE!
CLIMB ON MY BACK.
HURRY.
THE OTHER DRAGONS ARE BLIND WITH RAGE . . .
THEY'LL RIP US APART IF THEY CATCH US.
KAA
REEE! KREE!
RUMMBLE
KOON

KREE! RAAAAAAAH
HOLD TIGHT.
CRASH! KRAEE!
FLAP! FLAP! FLAP!
HERE THEY COME!

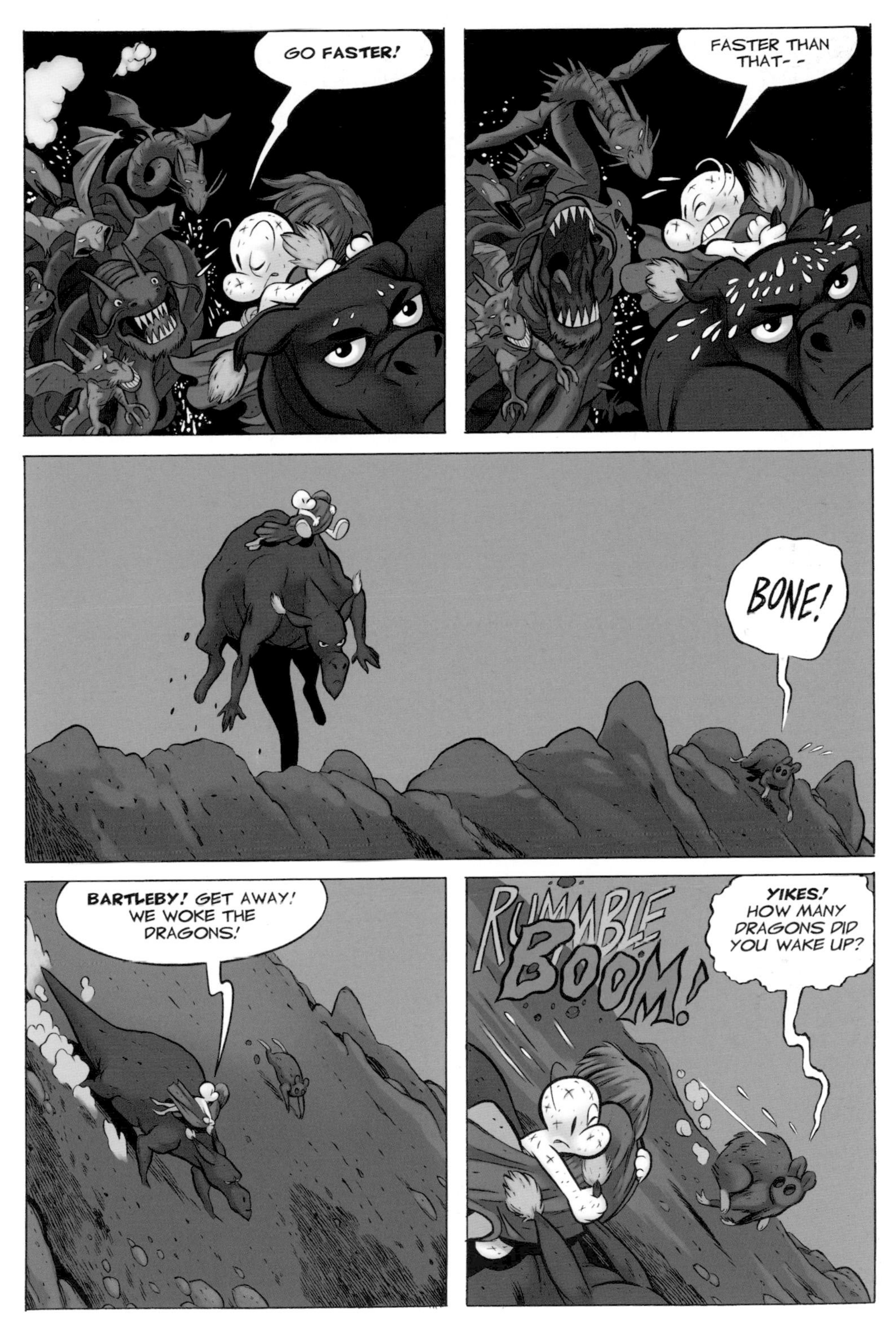
GO FASTER!
FASTER THAN THAT- -
BONE!
BARTLEBY! GET AWAY! WE WOKE THE DRAGONS!
RUMMBLE BOOM!
YIKES! HOW MANY DRAGONS DID YOU WAKE UP?

ALL OF THEM!
WAIT - - WHY AREN'T THEY BEHIND US? THE DRAGONS CHANGED DIRECTIONS - -
OH, NO! THEY'RE UNDERNEATH US!
RUN, BARTLEBY!
BOOM
KEERAAKK
ROAR

BONE
YOUR MAJESTY, PLEASE LET ME PUT A BANDAGE ON YOUR ARM AND CHEST...
QUEEN ROSE!
THE RAT CREATURES ARE REGROUPING AND THE FUNNEL CLOUD IS BEGINNING TO BUILD STRENGTH!
WHAT?
LOOK! THE CLOUD IS STILL CHURNING!
BUT THE LOCUSTS ARE DEAD. WHAT'S MOVING IT?
THERE IS SOMETHING INSIDE THE STORM...
SOMETHING VERY BIG.

SOMETHING BIG . . . ? THORN WARNED ME THAT THE LOCUST WAS SENDING MIM AGAINST US.
MIM? THE MAD QUEEN OF THE DRAGONS?!
EEAAAOOOOOO
IT'S HER! HEADMASTER, WARN YOUR PEOPLE THAT WE ARE STILL UNDER ATTACK!
YOUR MAJESTY!!
RAT CREATURES ARE ASCENDING THE NORTH SLOPE!
WHERE ARE THE PAWANS?
COMING UP THE SOUTHERN SLOPE.
WE'RE SURROUNDED!
THEY MUST KNOW YOU'RE HERE.
EVERYONE MOVE TOWARD THE TUNNEL! WE'RE LEAVING!
HELP ME GET LUCIUS TO HIS FEET - -
ROSE . . . LUCIUS IS DEAD.

LOOK OUT!
HERE THEY COME!

YOUR HIGHNESS!
COMING ACROSS THE PLAIN-- IT'S THE GREAT RED DRAGON!
HE'S CARRYING THORN AND BONE--
BUT WHAT'S THAT BEHIND THEM?

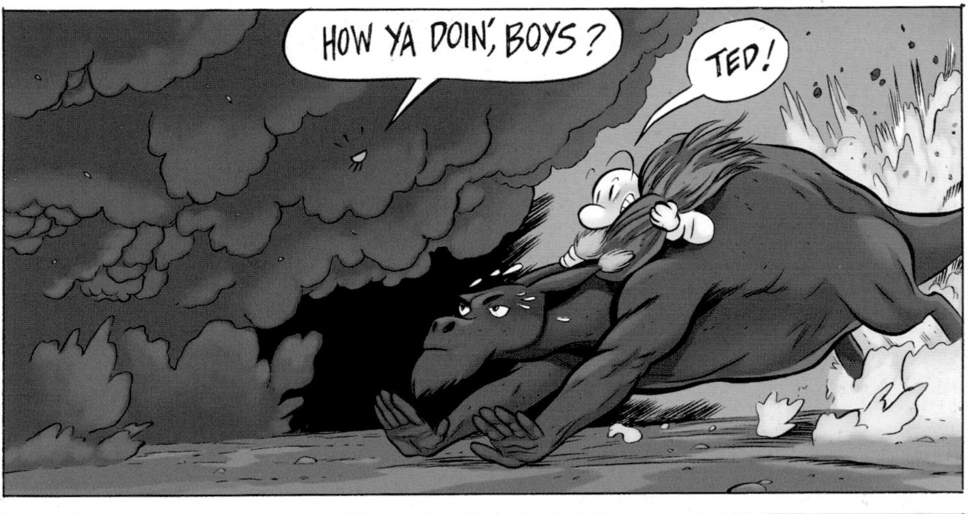
HOW YA DOIN', BOYS?
TED!

GRAN'MA'S UP ON SINNER'S ROCK. COULD USE SOME HELP.
ON IT.

THORN!
SSSS KRAAKK
GRAN'MA!
WHAT HAPPENED TO THE DRAGONS FOLLOWING US?
EVERYONE **HOLD ON TO SOMETHING** - -
BOOM

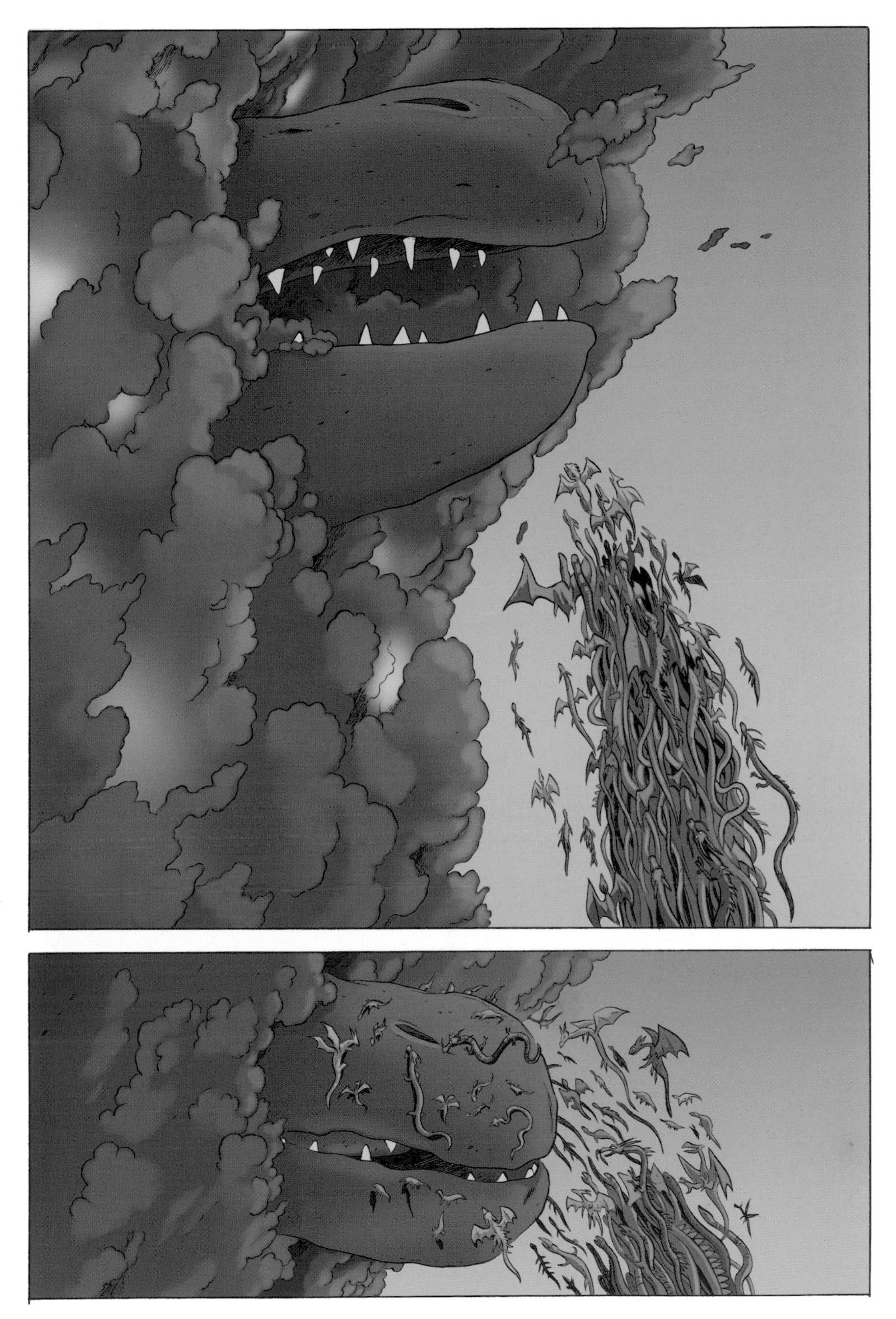

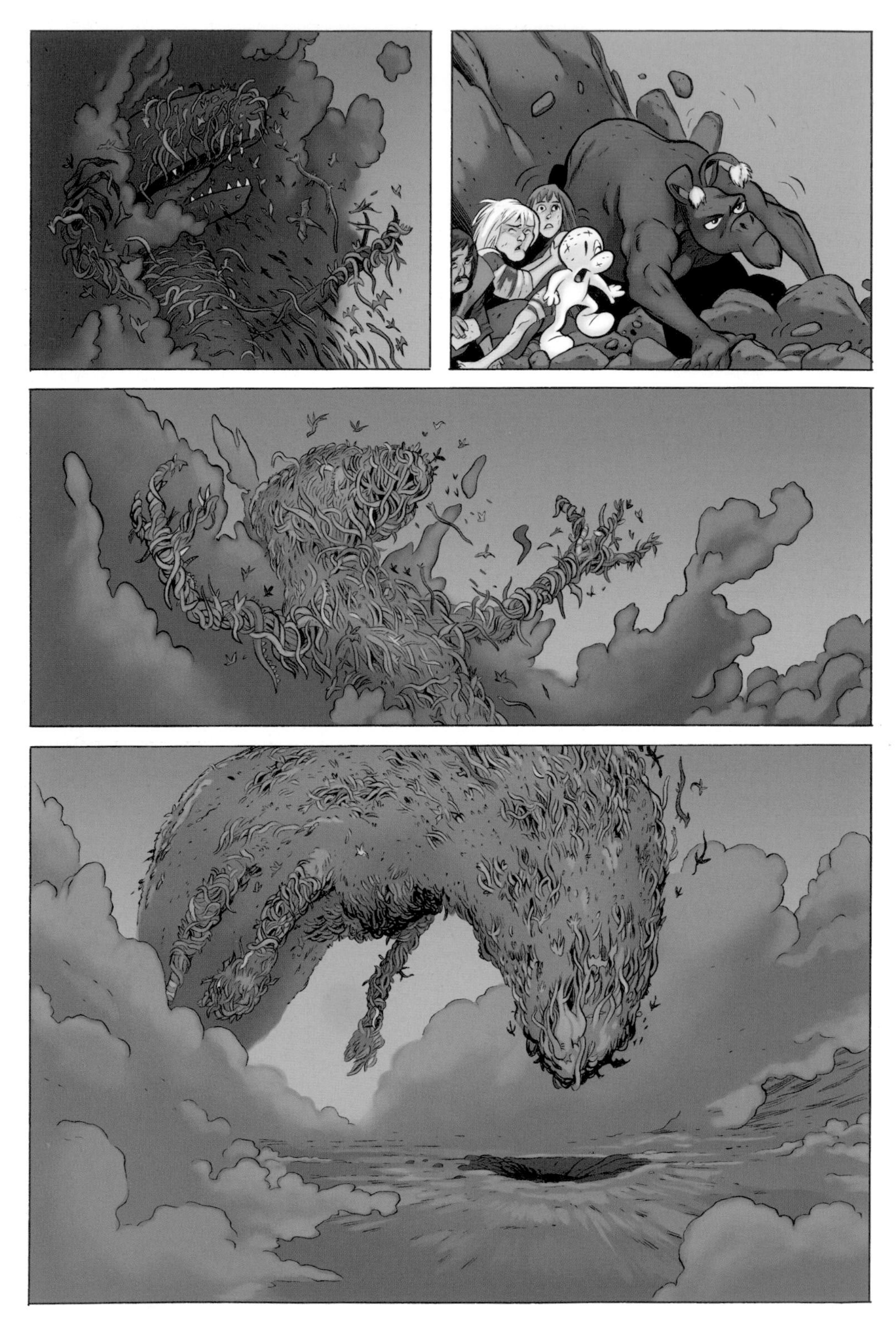

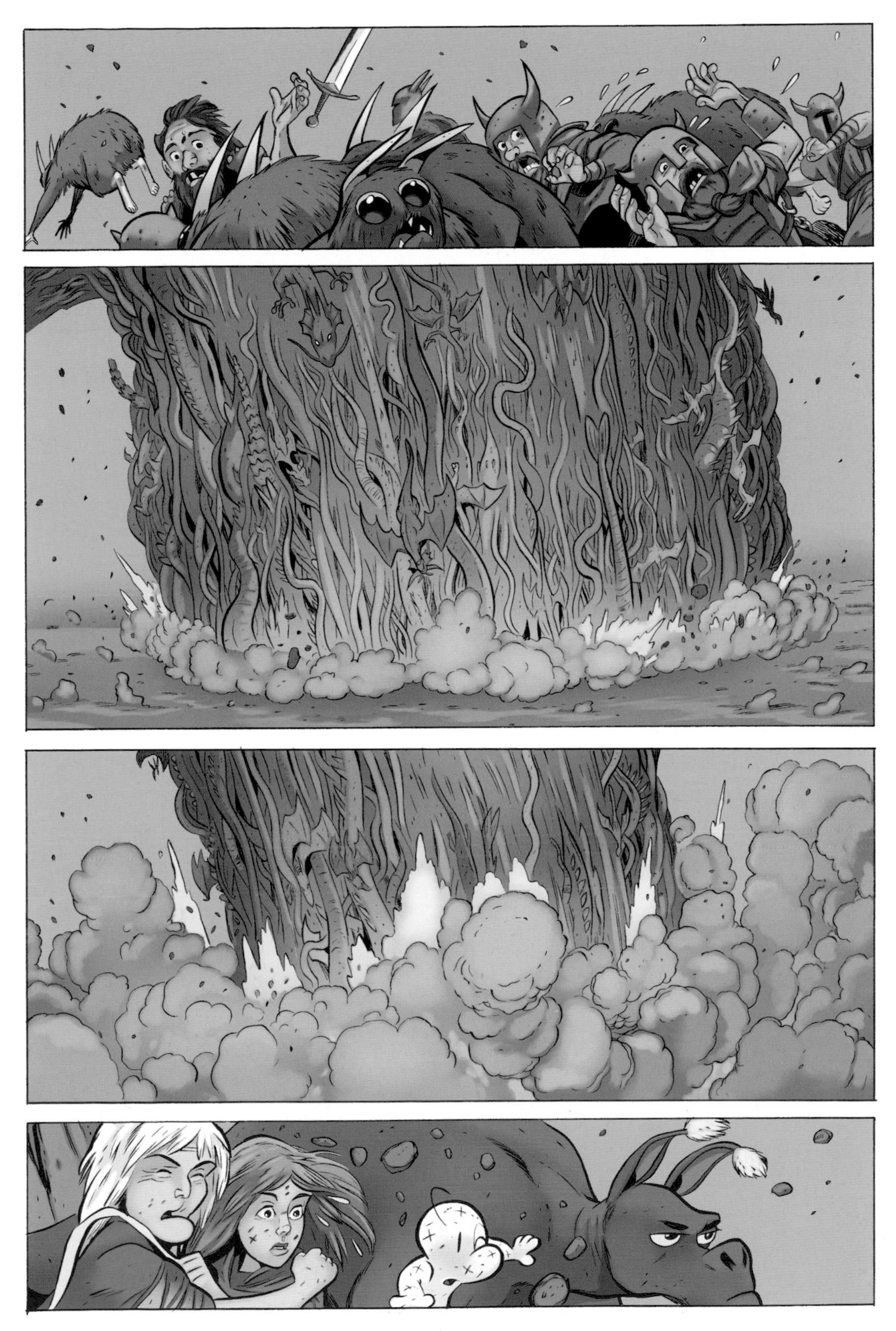

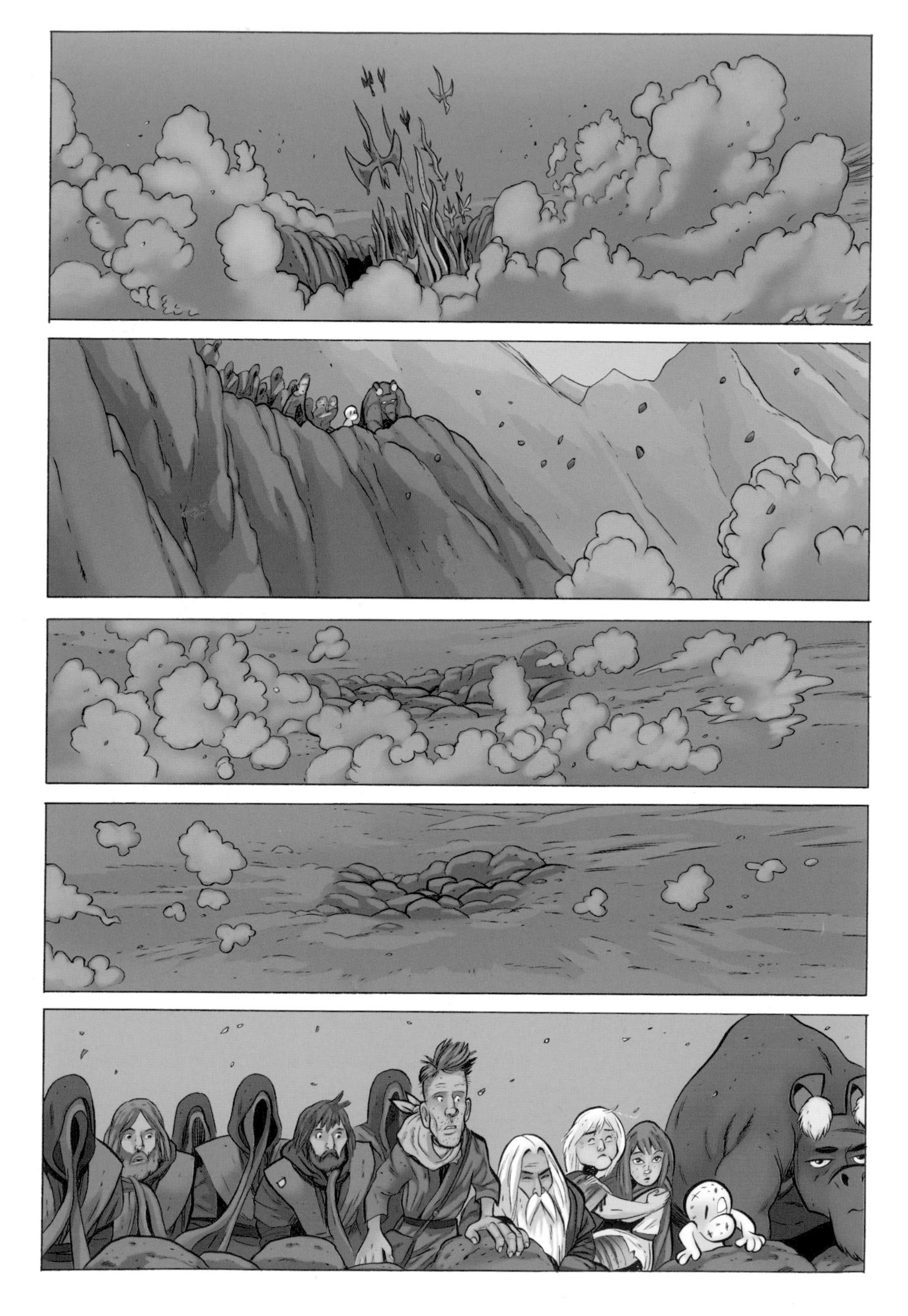

HEY!
WHAT ARE YOU GUYS DOIN' SITTIN' AROUND? THERE'S A **WAR** ON AN' I BROUGHT THE **RESERVES!**
ARE YA TAKIN' A **BREAK** - - WHERE'S THE ENEMY? WHERE'S THE RAT CREATURES?
Ohhh!
I MISSED THE WAR, DIDN'T I?
THE DRAGONS WE BROUGHT HERE **ENDED IT!**
TYPICAL. HOGGIN' ALL THE GLORY FOR YOURSELF! WELL, I'M STILL A HERO, YOU **GOT** THAT?
YES!
FONE BONE!

SOMETHING IS WRONG WITH GRAN'MA BEN--
GRAN'MA!

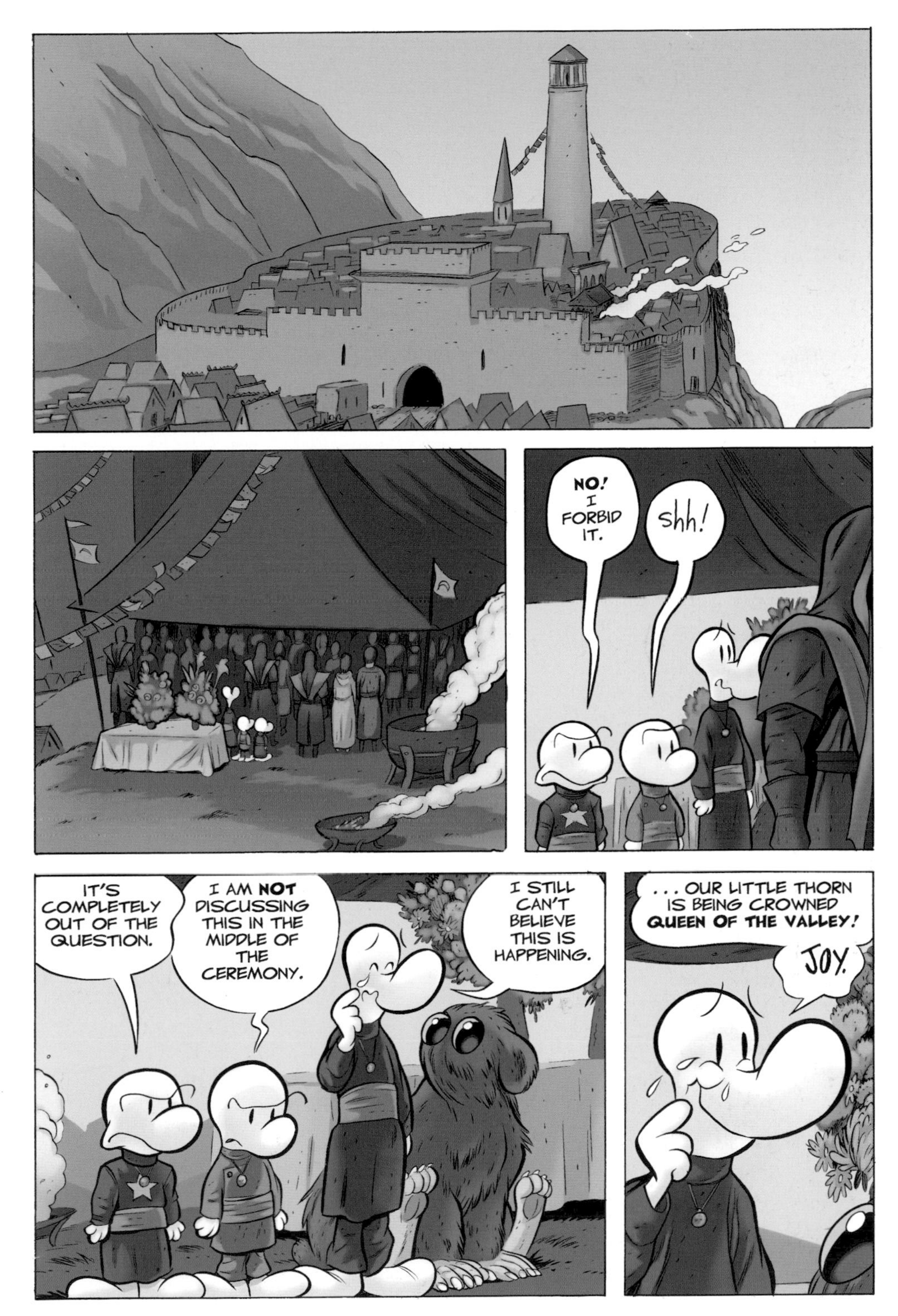
NO! I FORBID IT.
shh!
IT'S COMPLETELY OUT OF THE QUESTION.
I AM NOT DISCUSSING THIS IN THE MIDDLE OF THE CEREMONY.
I STILL CAN'T BELIEVE THIS IS HAPPENING.
. . . OUR LITTLE THORN IS BEING CROWNED QUEEN OF THE VALLEY!
JOY.

AND HER LEG IS HEALING NICELY, JUST LIKE YOUR EYE. I THINK TOUCHING THE CROWN OF HORNS HAD SOMETHING TO DO WITH YOUR SPEEDY **RECOVERIES.**
I DUNNO, BUT THE DRAGON GAVE US NEW TEETH MADE FROM THE SAME CRYSTAL THAT THE CROWN OF HORNS IS MADE OF. . . SEE?
THAT IS SO COOL.
WHO CARES! ARE YOU COMING BACK TO BONEVILLE WITH US OR NOT?
LEAVE HIM ALONE, PHONEY, HE DOESN'T HAVE TO DECIDE NOW. HE'S GOT THE WHOLE TRIP TO BARRELHAVEN TO THINK ABOUT IT.

I DON'T WANNA WAIT 'TIL WE GET TO BARRELHAVEN, SMILEY. THORN ASKED HIM TO STAY AND I WANNA KNOW **NOW!** ARE YOU GONNA HELP RULE THE KINGDOM OR ARE YOU COMIN' WITH **US?**
PHONCIBLE P. BONE, YOU ARE GOING TO SUPPORT YOUR COUSIN NO MATTER **WHAT** DECISION HE MAKES BECAUSE YOU **LOVE** HIM.
NOW, IN A COUPLE OF DAYS WE'RE GONNA GO WITH THORN AND GRAN'MA BEN TO LAY LUCIUS TO REST BESIDE THE OLD BARRELHAVEN TAVERN . . . FONE BONE CAN DECIDE WHEN WE GET THERE.
SIGH.
ALL RIGHT. I GUESS WHATEVER YOU WANT WILL BE OKAY WITH ME.
THAT'S BETTER. WE'RE BEHIND YOU A **HUNDRED PERCENT**, FONE BONE.

C'MON, PHONEY, CHEER UP! IT'S A BEAUTIFUL MORNING.
Bread thingies
IT'S TOO COLD TO TRAVEL.
LUCIUS LOVED THE LATE FALL. I THINK HE'D BE HAPPY TRAVELING TO THE NORTH WOODS THIS TIME OF YEAR.

THANK YOU FOR DOING THIS, DEAR.
WAIT!

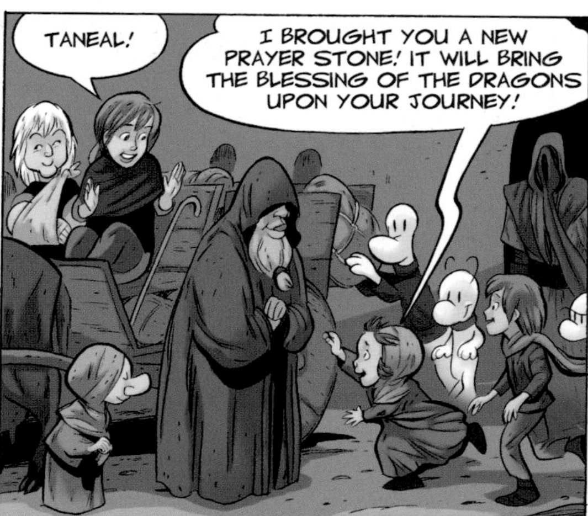
TANEAL!
I BROUGHT YOU A NEW PRAYER STONE! IT WILL BRING THE BLESSING OF THE DRAGONS UPON YOUR JOURNEY!

THANK YOU! I'LL BRING YOU SOMETHING FROM THE NORTH WHEN I RETURN.
MR. BONE! I HAVE BEGUN A NEW CARVING OF YOU AND BARTLEBY!
US? REALLY?
IT SHOWS HOW YOU HELPED SISTER THORN DEFEAT THE LOCUST AND BANISH THE GHOST CIRCLES. IT WILL BE FINISHED BY THE TIME YOU GET BACK.
I'M HONORED. I CAN'T WAIT TO SEE IT.
I HOPE WE HAVEN'T FORGOTTEN ANYTHING.
DON'T WORRY, YOUR HIGHNESS, EVERYTHING WILL BE FINE. MERMIE AND I WILL SEE TO THAT.
JUST IN CASE YOU CAN'T MAKE IT BACK BEFORE IT SNOWS, THE GREAT RED DRAGON HAS PROMISED TO HELP KEEP AN EYE ON THE KINGDOM.
BUT THAT WON'T BE A PROBLEM - - I HAVE READ THE SIGNS AND I PREDICT A MILD WINTER!
VERY GOOD. WE SHOULD START THEN.
BOYS?
ARE YOU GOING TO RIDE OR WALK ALONGSIDE?
I'LL WALK FOR A WHILE.

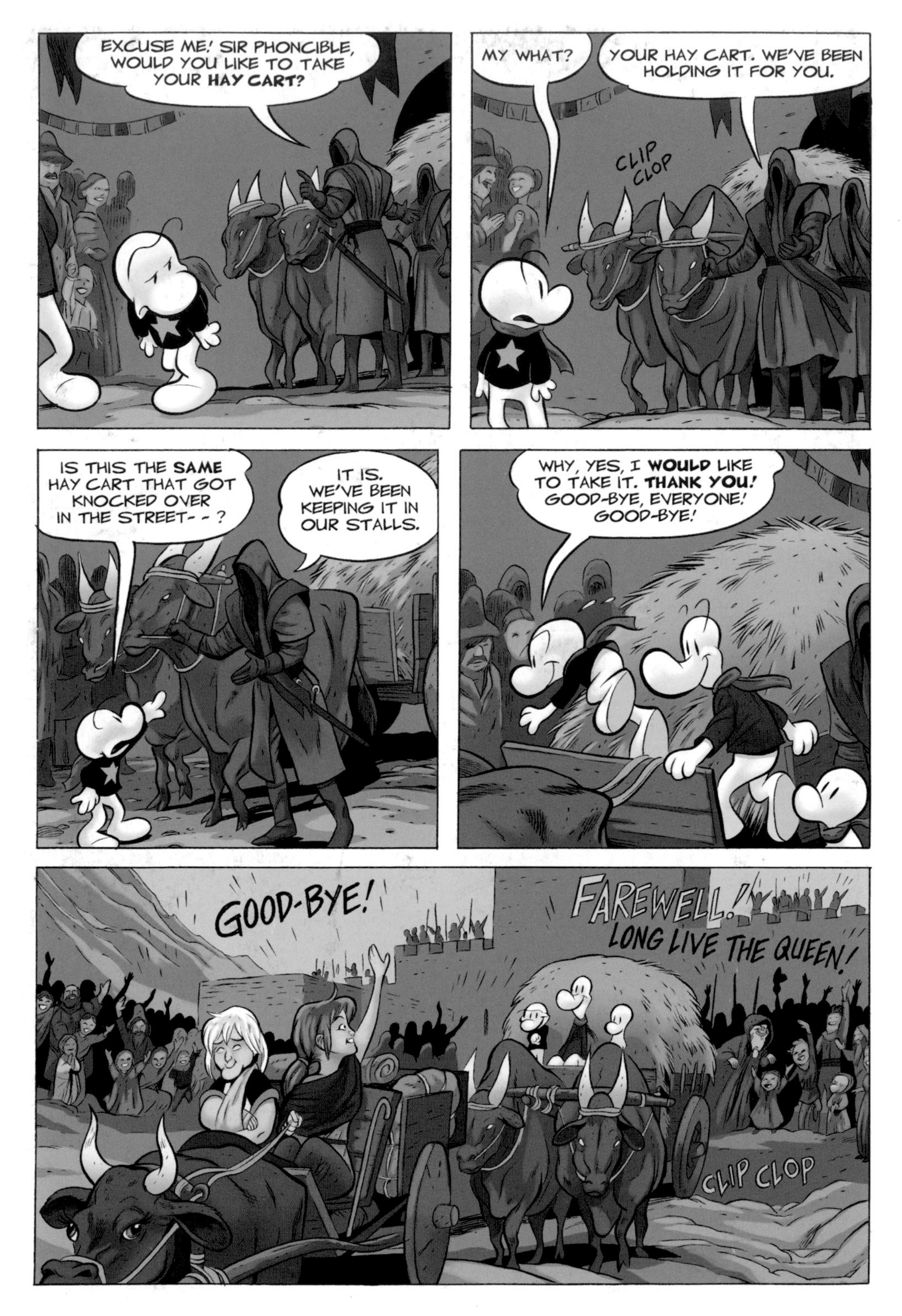
EXCUSE ME! SIR PHONCIBLE, WOULD YOU LIKE TO TAKE YOUR HAY CART?
MY WHAT?
YOUR HAY CART. WE'VE BEEN HOLDING IT FOR YOU.
CLIP CLOP
IS THIS THE SAME HAY CART THAT GOT KNOCKED OVER IN THE STREET- - ?
IT IS. WE'VE BEEN KEEPING IT IN OUR STALLS.
WHY, YES, I WOULD LIKE TO TAKE IT. THANK YOU! GOOD-BYE, EVERYONE! GOOD-BYE!
GOOD-BYE!
FAREWELL!
LONG LIVE THE QUEEN!
CLIP CLOP

SAY, DO YOU GUYS MIND IF WE STOP FOR A SECOND? I WANT TO CHECK SOMETHING REAL FAST...
GOTTA MAKE SURE ALL MY... HAY... IS HERE.
JUST CHECKING FOR MY HAY... AH, YES, HERE WE ARE...
SLAM!
I DON'T BELIEVE IT.
YES! LET'S RIDE, AMIGOS!
HOT DIGGETY-DOG! WHAT A BEAUTIFUL DAY FOR TRAVELING!

I THINK WE'RE ALMOST THERE, SMILEY- - THAT'S THE FAIRGROUNDS THROUGH THOSE TREES.
THE FAIRGROUNDS?! OH, BOY! THE LAST TIME I WAS AT THE FAIRGROUNDS WAS FOR THE GREAT COW RACE! REMEMBER THAT?
WOULD YOU SIT DOWN, PHONEY? YOU'VE BEEN FIDGETING THE ENTIRE TRIP!
I THOUGHT I SAW A SNOWFLAKE.
ENOUGH WITH THE SNOWFLAKES. WE'LL MAKE IT TO THE PASS BEFORE IT SNOWS.
TWO DAYS WE SPENT AT OLD MAN'S CAVE! WE'RE NEVER GONNA GET OUT OF THIS VALLEY!

PHONEY, GRAN'MA BEN HAS A LOT OF FRIENDS AT OLD MAN'S CAVE. AND LUCIUS WAS A HERO . . .
. . . PEOPLE NEEDED TIME TO SHOW THEIR RESPECT.
OKAY, OKAY. I'M JUST SAYING THERE'S ONLY SO MANY DAYS LEFT BEFORE IT SNOWS FOR REAL.
THE OLD TEACHER READ THE SIGNS AND PREDICTED A MILD WINTER - -
MY POINT EXACTLY! THAT GUY COULDN'T PREDICT A FALL IF HE WAS STEPPIN' ON A BANANA PEEL!
DID YOU SEE THAT? THAT WAS A FLAKE.
HELLO!
WENDELL! AN' LOOK WHO'S WITH HIM! IT'S EUCLID!

CAN YOU **BELIEVE** IT? HE WAS WAITING FOR ME WHEN I GOT BACK!
I WAS INSIDE A GHOST CIRCLE, BUT THEN ONE DAY I WOKE UP FROM A DEEP SLEEP AND IT WAS GONE!
YAY!
I UNDERSTAND THAT I HAVE **YOU** TO THANK . . . YOUR **MAJESTY.**
AND THAT GOES FOR YOU, TOO, LITTLE MASTER BONE.
OH, NO SWEAT.
HEY, EUCLID! YOU FORGOT SOMEONE.
THE REASON WE WALKED OUT TO MEET YOU IS BECAUSE A COUPLE OF MANGY RAT CREATURES HAVE BEEN SPOTTED SCROUNGING AROUND.
OH, NO! YOU THINK IT'S **OUR** TWO RAT CREATURES?
COULD BE. I HAD TO LET THEM GO ONCE THE NEW TREATY WAS SIGNED.
THEY'RE NOT SUCH BAD GUYS, REALLY.

IF IT **IS** THE SAME TWO, THEY'RE PROBABLY NOT DANGEROUS - - JUST LOOKING FOR SOMETHING TO EAT, BUT WE'LL KEEP OUR EYES OPEN.
THIS MUST BE LUCIUS.
WELCOME HOME, OLD FRIEND.
EVERYTHING'S READY. I SUPPOSE WE SHOULD GET HIM IN THE GROUND.

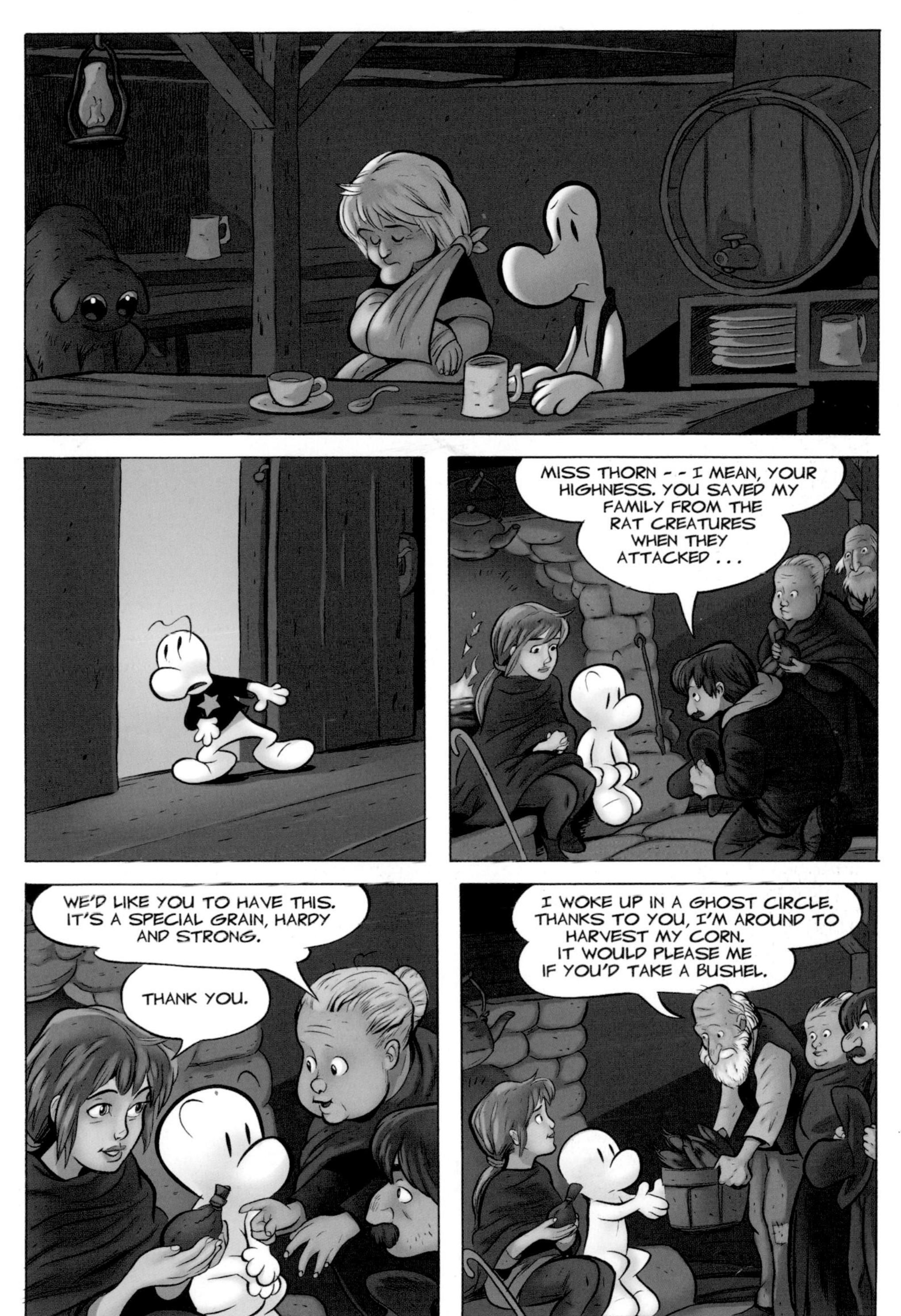
MISS THORN -- I MEAN, YOUR HIGHNESS. YOU SAVED MY FAMILY FROM THE RAT CREATURES WHEN THEY ATTACKED ...
WE'D LIKE YOU TO HAVE THIS. IT'S A SPECIAL GRAIN, HARDY AND STRONG.
THANK YOU.
I WOKE UP IN A GHOST CIRCLE. THANKS TO YOU, I'M AROUND TO HARVEST MY CORN. IT WOULD PLEASE ME IF YOU'D TAKE A BUSHEL.

SHE'S GOING TO HAVE TO GET USED TO THIS KIND OF TREATMENT.
HOW IS SHE HANDLING HER NEW RESPONSIBILITIES AS MONARCH?
SHE HAS THE BEST ADVISORS. MERMIE AND MY OLD TEACHER PRACTICALLY RAN THE KINGDOM FOR THE LAST FIFTEEN YEARS.
THE ONLY PROBLEM IS WE CAN'T FIND THE CITY'S TREASURE THAT TARSIL HID. BUT WE'LL HAVE TO - - WE CAN'T RUN THE KINGDOM WITHOUT IT.
HEY! IT SMELLS LIKE SNOW OUTSIDE.
WHAT DO YOU MEAN?
IT'S COLD AN' SMELLS LIKE IT'S GONNA SNOW. C'MON, WE GOTTA LEAVE.
BUT WE STILL HAVE TO GO TO GRAN'MA'S FARMHOUSE - - AND FONE BONE HASN'T DECIDED IF HE'S STAYING OR NOT.
RRR.
TELL HIM TO HURRY UP.

YOU KNOW, ROSE, YOU CAN STAY HERE. EUCLID AND I HAVE BEEN WORKING PRETTY HARD TO REBUILD THIS PLACE, AND THE NORTH BEDROOMS ARE FINISHED.
OH, YOU'VE BOTH DONE A WONDERFUL JOB, WENDELL! LUCIUS WOULD BE PROUD, BUT I'D LIKE TO SPEND A LITTLE TIME AT THE OLD HOUSE BEFORE THORN AND I GO BACK TO ATHEIA.
ME, TOO! I CAN'T WAIT TO SEE THE PLACE!
BOY, YOU SHOULD SEE ALL THE CORN AND GRAIN AN' STUFF THE TOWNSFOLK GAVE US.
WHERE'S PHONEY?
HE'S STILL WORRIED WE'RE GONNA GET SNOWED IN FOR THE WINTER.
The Barrel Haven
AAH!

SLAM!
GUYS! GUYS!! I SAW A SNOW-FLAKE!
WHAT CAN ONE SNOWFLAKE HURT?
WHUMP!
The Barrel Haven
OH, YEAH. SORRY.

BONE
WE'RE BACK! AND WAIT'LL YOU SEE THE TREE THAT BONE AND I FOUND!
YOU GOT A TREE, THORN? YOU GUYS USE A TREE TO CELEBRATE TH' WINTER SOLSTICE?!
OF COURSE WE DO, SMILEY! BRINGING AN EVERGREEN INTO THE HOUSE ON THE SHORTEST, DARKEST DAY OF WINTER IS A VERY OLD TRADITION!
BOY, IS THAT A RELIEF! NOW WE HAVE SOME-WHERE TO PUT OUR PRIZES!
LEMME MAKE SURE THERE'S ENOUGH ROOM!

THE TREE REPRESENTS LIFE IN THE DEAD OF WINTER.
HOW DO YOU CELEBRATE BACK IN BONEVILLE?
GEE. . . I DUNNO.
HEY, PHONEY! DO WE CELEBRATE TH' WINTER SOLSTICE IN BONEVILLE??
YEAH.
BUT FOR DIFFERENT REASONS.
DIFFERENT REASONS . . . DIFFERENT NAMES . . . IT ALL COMES DOWN TO TH' SAME THING - - BUSINESS PICKS UP, AN' I MAKE A LOTTA MONEY!
I LOVE THIS HOLIDAY!
THAT IS . . . I USED TO. NOW I JUST SIT HERE QUIETLY - - DYING INSIDE, LIKE DECAYING LEAVES BENEATH THE SNOW.
HMMF. YOU'RE NOT THAT QUIET.
C'MON! LET'S PLAY SOME INSTRUMENTS!
AS LONG AS WE'RE GONNA MAKE MUSIC, IT DON'T MATTER TO ME IF WE CELEBRATE FOR DIFFERENT REASONS!

HEY, BONE! WHERE YOU GOIN'?
I'LL BE RIGHT BACK, GRAN'MA!
HELLO?
HEY, GUYS! C'MON OUT! I KNOW YOU'RE AROUND HERE SOMEWHERE!
AH! THERE YOU ARE!
AAAARRRGH!
PREPARE TO TASTE INSTANT, BLOODY DEATH, SMALL MAMMAL!

NOT THIS TIME, GUYS! TODAY IS DIFFERENT!
CHING!
PIPING HOT QUICHE!
FOR YOU!
PEACE ON EARTH, FELLAS!
WHAT DO YOU SUPPOSE THAT WAS ALL ABOUT?
WHY QUESTION IT? IT'S JUST SOME RITUAL TH' HUMANS GO THROUGH EVERY YEAR.
EAT YOUR QUICHE.

BONE
FINALLY!
YES!
IT'S SPRING!
LET'S GO, PEOPLE! WE GOT SOME LEAVIN' TO DO...

TIME'S UP, FONE BONE! ARE YOU STAYIN' OR COMING WITH SMILEY AN' ME?
WELL, ACTUALLY...
A-HEM
NOW, I DON'T WANT TO SWAY YOU, BUT WHEN I GET HOME TO BONEVILLE, I'M GOIN' TO CORN DOG HUT™.
ooh! CORN DOGS --
SMILEY! ARE YOU TRYING TO TEMPT FONE BONE WITH BONEVILLE DELICACIES?
WHAT? NO! I'M JUST SAYIN'... PIZZA-IN-A-CUP™!
YUM YUM YUM!
WELL, HERE, HE'LL BE RICH AND FAMOUS -- IF HE RULES THE KINGDOM, HE'LL HAVE POWER!
NO FAIR! NO ONE CAN RESIST THAT!
IF HE STAYS HE'LL NEVER HAVE BIG JOHNSON'S PISTACHIO-PECAN-CASHEW ICE CREAM™ AGAIN!
HEY, GUYS. I APPRECIATE EVERYONE'S HELP, BUT I'VE ALREADY MADE UP MY MIND...

I WANT TO GO BACK TO BONEVILLE.
I KNOW. IT'S OKAY.
ARE YOU SURE? I MEAN, YOU HAVE A WHOLE NEW LIFE NOW -- YOU'RE **QUEEN**, AN' YOU'RE GONNA HAVE A MILLION THINGS TO DO --
YOU DON'T HAVE TO EXPLAIN, FONE BONE. I KNOW HOW MUCH YOU LOVE YOUR COUSINS.
BESIDES, I KIND OF GUESSED YOU WERE LEAVING WHEN YOU PACKED YOUR BAG THIS MORNING.
YOU KNOW WHATEVER YOU DECIDE IS OKAY WITH ME.
HOORAY!
YAY!
I'LL GO START THE COWS!
HITCH OL' BESSIE UP, WE'LL RIDE WITH YOU TO THE PASS.

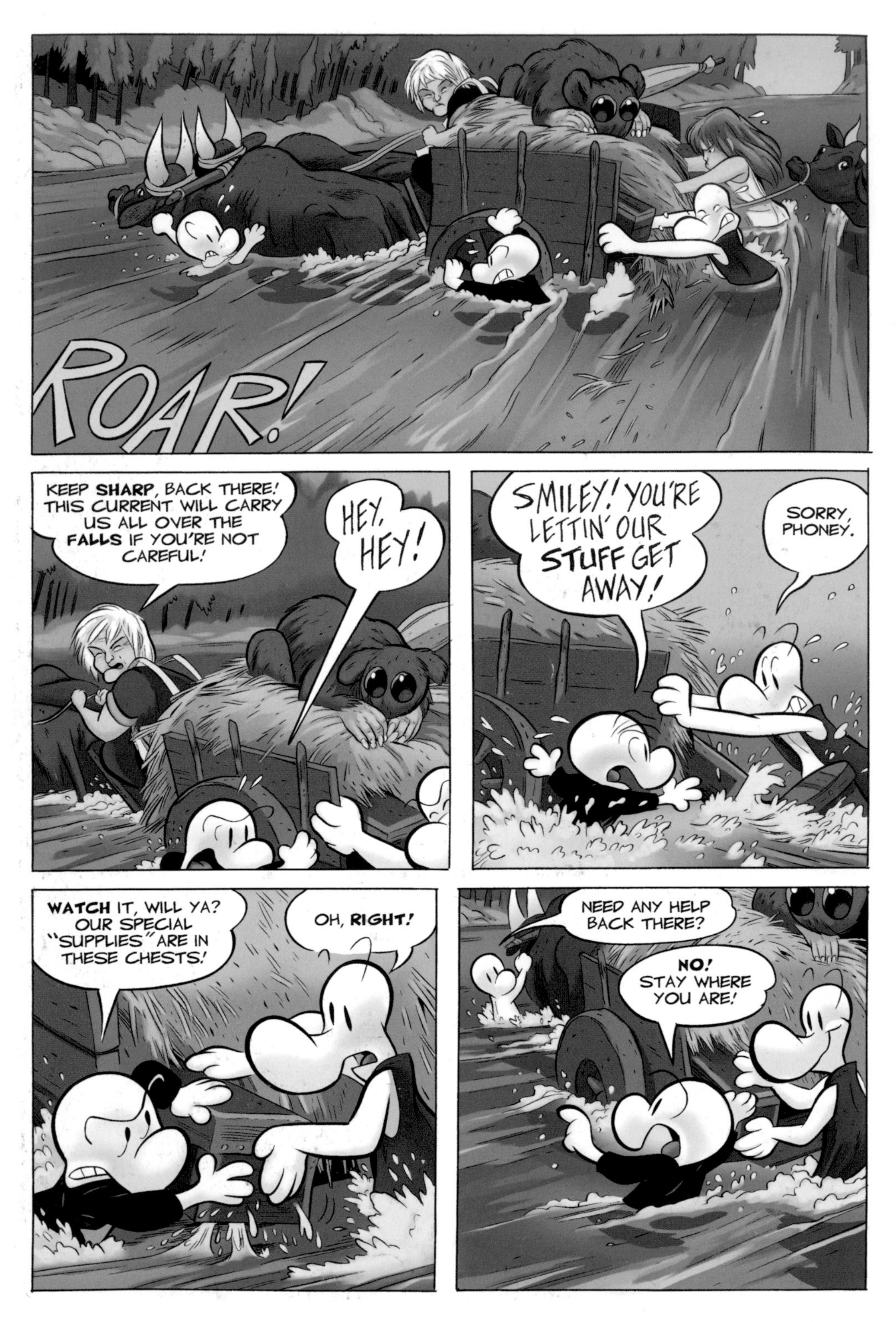
ROAR!
KEEP SHARP, BACK THERE! THIS CURRENT WILL CARRY US ALL OVER THE FALLS IF YOU'RE NOT CAREFUL!
HEY, HEY!
SMILEY! YOU'RE LETTIN' OUR STUFF GET AWAY!
SORRY, PHONEY.
WATCH IT, WILL YA? OUR SPECIAL "SUPPLIES" ARE IN THESE CHESTS!
OH, RIGHT!
NEED ANY HELP BACK THERE?
NO! STAY WHERE YOU ARE!

THINK YOU CAN HANDLE IT FROM HERE?
SORRY, MAN, THE CART HIT A ROCK OR SOMETHING.
JUST PUSH!
EENH!
RUSTLE!
HEY- - I JUST SAW SOMETHING MOVE UNDER THE TREES!
I SAW IT, TOO.
PSST! GUYS! GET OUT THE SPEARS!

RUSTLE! RUSTLE!
HEY, GUYS! IT'S ME AN' DRAGON!
HEY.
WHEW.
FOLLOW US.

HOW MUCH FARTHER?
WE'RE HERE.
THIS IS IT, BART! WE'RE ON OUR WAY TO YOUR NEW HOME!
JOY!
AND NOT A MOMENT TOO SOON . . .

HATE TO RUN, YOU CRAZY CRACKERS, BUT I'VE GOT AN EMPIRE TO REBUILD! HERO'S WELCOMES, TICKER TAPE PARADES - - THAT KIND OF STUFF!
GOOD-BYE, GRAN'MA BEN. THANK YOU FOR EVERYTHING.
TAKE CARE OF YOURSELF, BONE.
WELL, DRAGON, I GUESS I'LL SEE YOU AROUND...
YOU, TOO, TED.
LATER DAYS, BONE.
TRAVEL AT NIGHT, FONE BONE, KEEP THE SUNSET ON YOUR LEFT, NORTH STAR ON YOUR RIGHT. YOU'LL FIND YOUR WAY.
AND THANKS FOR THE HELP, KID.
I PACKED YOU A LITTLE BASKET OF BISCUITS AND HONEY. I SAVED IT UNTIL NOW BECAUSE . . . I WAS HOPING YOU'D CHANGE YOUR MIND.

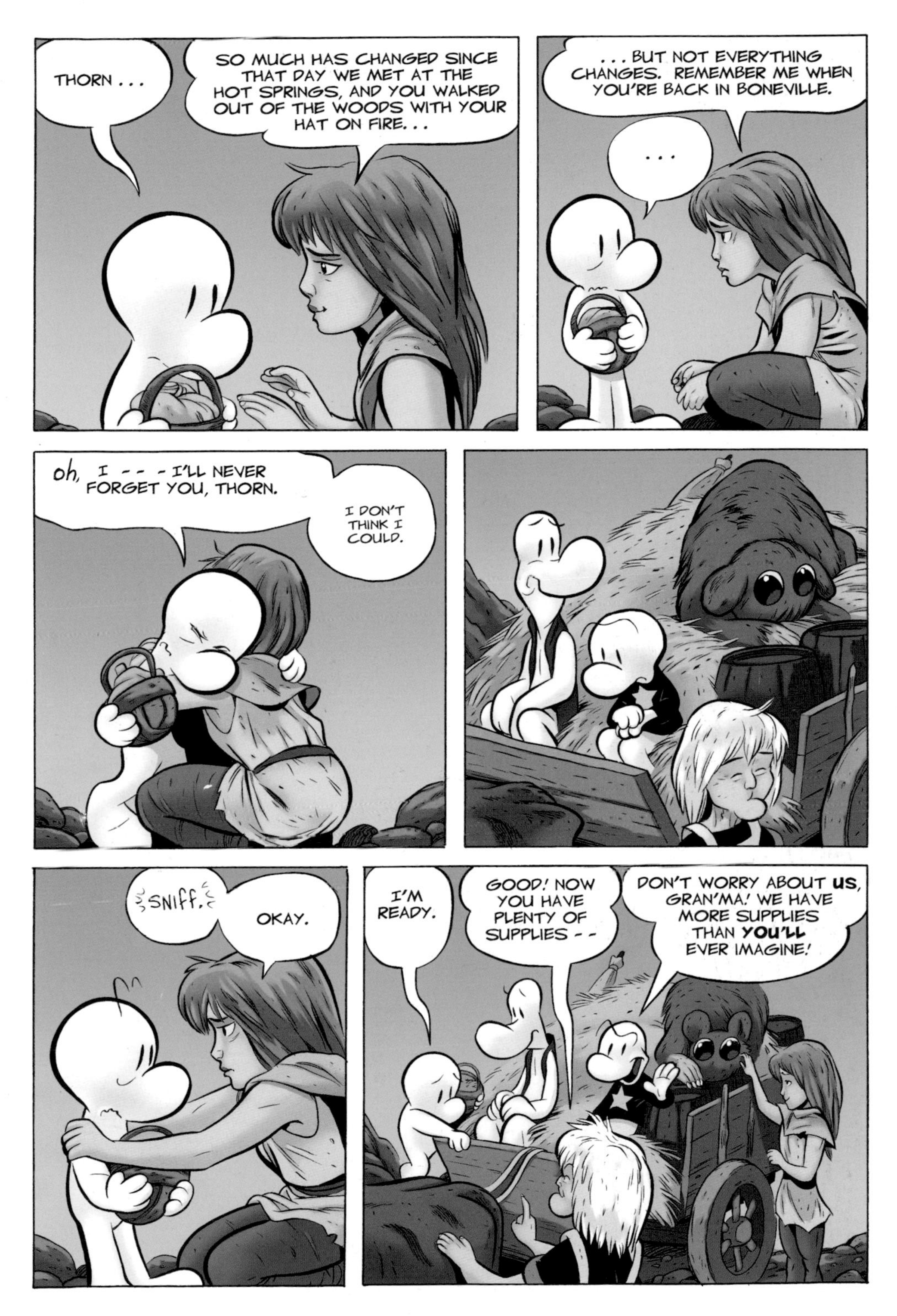
THORN . . .
SO MUCH HAS CHANGED SINCE THAT DAY WE MET AT THE HOT SPRINGS, AND YOU WALKED OUT OF THE WOODS WITH YOUR HAT ON FIRE. . .
. . . BUT NOT EVERYTHING CHANGES. REMEMBER ME WHEN YOU'RE BACK IN BONEVILLE.
. . .
oh, I - - - I'LL NEVER FORGET YOU, THORN.
I DON'T THINK I COULD.
SNIFF.
OKAY.
I'M READY.
GOOD! NOW YOU HAVE PLENTY OF SUPPLIES - -
DON'T WORRY ABOUT US, GRAN'MA! WE HAVE MORE SUPPLIES THAN YOU'LL EVER IMAGINE!

YOU DO?
OH, YEAH, WE'RE LOADED. WE'VE GOT FOUR TREASURE CHESTS FULL OF THOSE HARD, STALE BREAD-THINGIES!
WAIT. WHAT DID YOU SAY?
WE'VE GOT PLENTY OF THOSE HARD, STUFFED BREAD-THINGIES! THERE ALMOST WASN'T ROOM IN THE CART, BUT GRAN'MA HELPED EMPTY OUT THE TREASURE CHESTS - -
YOU EMPTIED OUT THE TREASURE?!
- - AND REFILLED THEM WITH ENOUGH BREAD-THINGIES TO LAST ALL THE WAY ACROSS THE DESERT!
AAH!
DON'T FEEL BAD, PHONCIBLE. HERE, HAVE SOME GOLD COINS - - THEY'RE THE ONES WITH YOUR FACE STAMPED ON THEM. NO ONE AROUND HERE WANTS 'EM ANYWAY!
A FEW COINS? I'M RUINED.
AND ON THAT NOTE . . . GIDDIYUP, DOGGIES!
GOOD-BYE, BONES! HAVE A SAFE JOURNEY!

GOOD-BYE!
GOOD-BYE!
CLIPCLOP CLIP
CLOP CLIP · CLOP

SIGH.
I DON'T EVEN LIKE HARD, STUFFED BREAD-THINGIES.
BETTER LEARN TO LIKE 'EM. THEY'RE THE ONLY FOOD ON BOARD.
FINE. HAND ME ONE.
GIMME A GOLD COIN FIRST.
WHAT?!
OH, GIVE HIM A GOLD COIN, PHONEY. WE'RE OUT IN THE MIDDLE OF THE DESERT.
The End
J.

TANEAL'S SCULPTURE, QUEEN'S SQUARE, ATHEIA

About JEFF SMITH

JEFF SMITH was born and raised in the American Midwest and learned about cartooning from comic strips, comic books, and watching animated shorts on TV. After four years of drawing comic strips for The Ohio State University's student newspaper and co-founding Character Builders animation studio in 1986, Smith launched the comic book *BONE* in 1991. Between *BONE* and other comics projects, Smith spends much of his time on the international guest circuit promoting comics and the art of graphic novels.

More about *BONE*

An instant classic when it first appeared in the U.S. as an underground comic book in 1991, *BONE* has since garnered 38 international awards and sold millions of copies in 15 languages. Now, Scholastic's GRAPHIX imprint is publishing full-color graphic novel editions of the nine-book *BONE* series.

Look for the exciting prequel to the amazing *BONE* series, *ROSE*, written by Jeff Smith and illustrated by award-winning artist Charles Vess.

OTHER GRAPHIC NOVELS FROM SCHOLASTIC

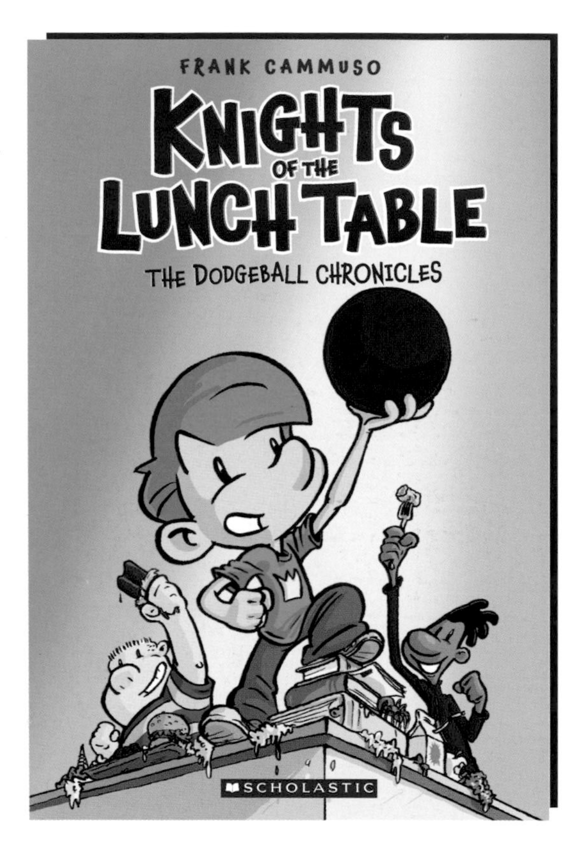

BEHOLD!
Artie King!
Ordinary hero!

KNIGHTS OF THE LUNCH TABLE
By Frank Cammuso

Artie King just wants to ease into life at Camelot Middle School. He's got new lunch buddies and a cool science teacher, but then there's the scary principal and Joe and the Horde, the brawny bullies who rule the school. The real trouble starts when Artie opens an old locker full of mysterious stuff, and Artie and his friends are challenged to a do-or-die dodgeball game. Losers get creamed!

Dreaming of Harvestar

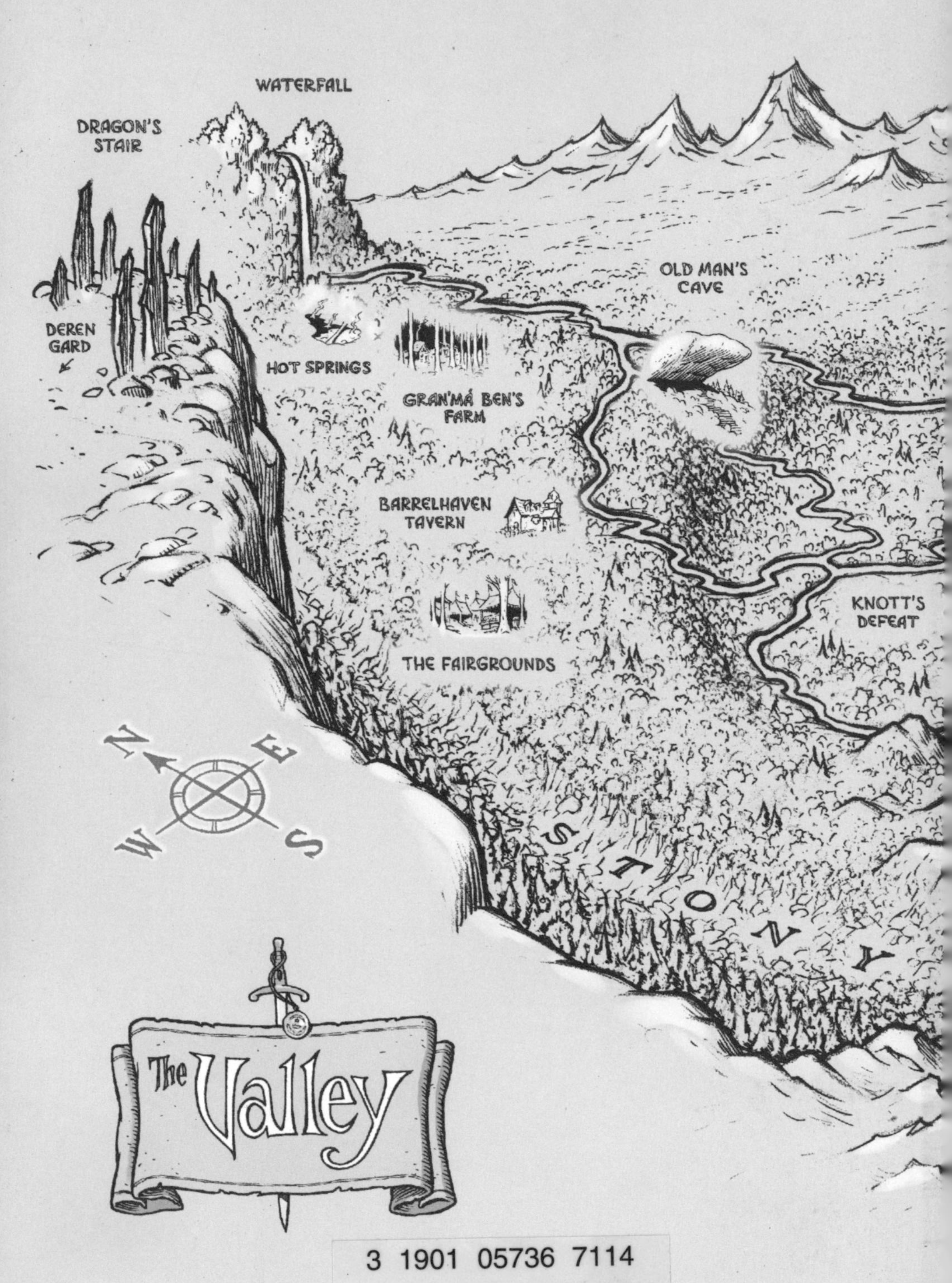
WATERFALL
DRAGON'S STAIR
DEREN GARD
HOT SPRINGS
GRAN'MA BEN'S FARM
OLD MAN'S CAVE
BARRELHAVEN TAVERN
KNOTT'S DEFEAT
THE FAIRGROUNDS
N
E
W
S
STONY
The Valley